Tales of the Old Detective
AND OTHER BIG FAT LIES

☼

ALSO BY PHILIP AUSTIN:

Roller Maidens from Outer Space *(Epic Records)*

WITH DAVID OSSMAN:

In the Next World, You're On Your Own *(Columbia Records)*

WITH THE FIRESIGN THEATRE:

Waiting for the Electrician or Someone Like Him
How Can You Be in Two Places at Once When You're Not Anywhere
 at All
Don't Crush That Dwarf, Hand Me the Pliers
I Think We're All Bozos on This Bus
Dear Friends
Not Insane or Anything You Want To
The Tale of the Giant Rat of Sumatra
Everything You Know Is Wrong *(Columbia Records)*

Just Folks: A Firesign Chat *(Butterfly Records)*

Nick Danger in The Case of the Missing Shoe
Fighting Clowns
Shakespeare's Lost Comedie (Anythynge You Want To)
Lawyer's Hospital
Nick Danger in the Three Faces of Al
Give Me Immortality or Give Me Death
Boom Dot Bust
Bride of Firesign *(Rhino Records)*

Hot Shorts *(Pioneer Artists)*

Nick Danger in the Case of the Missing Yolk *(Pacific Arts)*

Eat or Be Eaten *(Mercury Records)*

Back from the Shadows *(Mobile Fidelity Sound Lab)*

All Things Firesign *(Artemis Records)*

Tales of the Old Detective and Other Big Fat Lies

BY PHILIP AUSTIN

with illustrations by BRUCE LITZ

BEAR MANOR MEDIA

Published in the USA by:
BearManor Media
1317 Edgewater Dr #110
Orlando, FL 32804
www.BearManorMedia.com

The Firesign Theatre's website is firesigntheatre.com

Paperback ISBN 978-1-62933-820-0
Case ISBN 978-1-62933-821-7

BearManor Media, Orlando, Florida
Printed in the United States of America

Cover design and illustrations by Bruce Litz
Edited by Taylor Jessen
Layout by Robbie Adkins, adkinsconsult.com

First Edition

Contents

✧

Introduction
Where There's Jackalope, There's Hope

I was lucky enough to live with and love a man who had a vast imagination and sense of humor. In the most ordinary place he could dream up an alternative universe.

Always talking to and for animals, he had complete lives for squirrels in Central Park, marmots in the Sierras, ravens in the desert or seals in the Sound. Our dogs were legends...

The theatre albums and radio shows with the FST were also legends.

These are his city stories. Los Angeles, Lost Angels.

I hope they turn your ordinary day into something special.

I found this in a notebook:

"Honey" she'd say
"Yeah what" I'd say
"Tell me a story"
"No"
"Yes, tell me a story"
"I don't know any stories"
"Yes you do"
"Well..."
"What!"
"OK, this is a story about a pika who lives up the cliff..."

Oona Austin

.

Tales of the Old Detective
AND OTHER BIG FAT LIES

✧

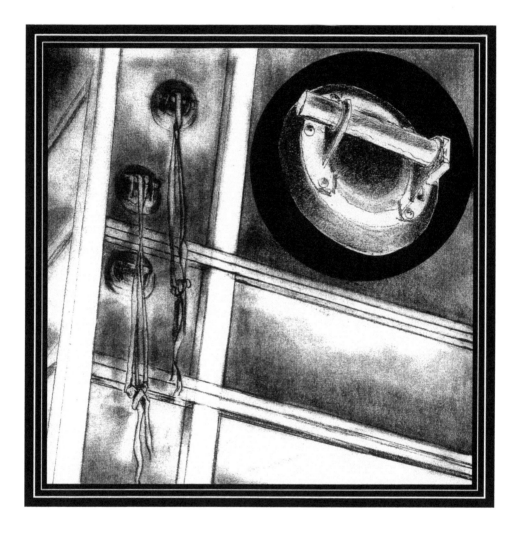

The Precipice of Angels

✿

NEW YORK CITY, *1ST DAY*

Received, a secret but all-too modest grant from the Institute des Boulevardistes in Paris. A mysterious call to the pay phone in the lobby of my horrible building, a muffled voice, directions, and finally a package of currency found in Central Park at the prearranged drop point, the location of which moves daily depending upon the vagaries of a troop of small parrots. Changed into anonymous American bills, the amount is scarcely enough to purchase supplies and necessaries for the adventure, but I am embarked. I am full of joy, I think. I need yet more money to afford the trip across the continent to California, which is a far place away. Now it becomes imperative that I disappear completely. I have left my sad apartment and carefully let it be known among my few friends and fewer parole officers that I am off to remote Nova

Scotia to tend a dying father whose existence I have carefully manufactured since my last arrest some years ago. I will sleep in the park and make phone calls from public booths, maintain my disguise and cover my tracks. At least it is still mild here and the weather my friend. Still no word from Kolmondegfar in Brussels as to route confirmation and the necessary (but secret) authorizations. These are slow in coming, I am afraid, largely because of the unfortunate experience of the Anglo-Dutch combined expedition of '84 on the south wall of this same thoroughfare, with its disastrous public displays and humiliations as well as the several deaths of local supply bearers, few Californians of that time having the necessary skills on polished granite and plate glass. My choice of the north wall suffers as well for the deaths of Gregg and Mitsubi—roped together as they were—and the unfortunate arrest and trial of Sir Jim Ashton-Whuippy. Still, for a lone climber, without oxygen, and without the need for supply bearers, one would think the proper authorizations might be more quickly granted. Mine will be the first solo climb, the third of any kind attempted on the north wall and, God willing, the first to succeed. I am paid up on dues to the Institute, I note, and as well my secret insurance and I am not unknown, my solo lateral ascent of Michigan Avenue in Chicago last year the matter of an extensive and secret article in the secret magazine of our secret sport. Might they yet deny me?

8TH DAY

Authorizations granted! I saw the pin stuck in the telephone pole on East 62nd and went to the drop point at the coded time and there were my permissions. I read, memorized and destroyed them. My heart is racing as I write this today, a fine day in the park by the little castle. The parrots are gone. There is a soft breeze and blowing clouds above, the radios of sunbathers blending into a gentle wash of nothing at all. My way is clear. I have taken three days of work as a coal miner to earn the airfare to the West coast. Temporary coal mining assignments are hard to come by, but I am with a good agency: Kelly Guys on West 45th and Broadway, just off Times Square.

LOS ANGELES—12TH DAY

Flew to the south of California today, high above the twisting hills with turquoise swimming pools inset like gems. I am disguised, of course, and have no problem with the nervous task of collecting my baggage. I think that people see climbing equipment as innocent here in the West, where there is a great traffic in mountaineering the Sierras and Rockies. To me and my kind all this is anathema. Vertical ascents and their happy conquerors are an urban lateralist's sworn enemies.

What a strange city Los Angeles is. Of first concern, it is quite low to the ground, understandable in a region of nearly constant earthquakes. In our sport, perversely, greater height on a route has come to be considered a bit of a cheat as it inevitably guarantees some secrecy for the climber. The over-used New York-style high routes have lately fallen out of favor, replaced by the seductive dangers unseen low-altitude horizon climbing along the broad avenues of these sun-washed cities of the American Southwest. For myself, intent upon a world record, the sheer length of a boulevard where I can find the prescribed distance with few apartments or houses or tracts of parkland is paramount. Wilshire Boulevard fits the bill. And, as well, it is a route with just enough height at correct intervals to guarantee lack of discovery in the daylight hours, when I must sleep at higher camps. Beside falling, of course, my greatest fear is discovery by a vengeful police force whose members have reportedly vowed to a man to stop boulevardists in our attempts since the celebrated acquittal of Sir Jim Ashton-Whuippy.

13TH DAY

Found lodging near the Boulevard itself in an unostentatious hotel—the Arms—just off Shrub Jay Avenue, using a name I will not set down even here. Am taking some days now to establish this sunny little suite of two rooms as a base supply camp, carefully secreting items and storing them within. It is actually quite pleasant here and from this second story I have a fine view of what will be my starting point where Kangaroux Avenue crosses busy Wilshire Boulevard. Purchased a bicycle and have quickly got the hang of it. Today a police car seemed to follow me as I rode the thing back from Westwood, its childish basket filled with dried food supplies purchased from A-16 Mountaineering, but I think I am overly fearful. However, is well to be cautious. I am too well known—should they check fingerprints—for me to claim to be merely a vertical climber gathering supplies for a foray in the nearby Sierras. Still, there has not been a celebrated arrest of any in our sport in this great city for some years and the whole matter of the trial of Ashton-Whuippy seems quite forgotten.

14TH DAY

Wilshire Boulevard might seem unimpressive when compared with the dizzying heights of the Avenues of New York or the intricate changes in lateral direction found in the older cities of Europe, but it is wonderful all the same. My route will encompass seventy blocks in total and therefore some sixty-nine side-street crossings. As well, the preponderance of slick facades, the jarring disparity in elevations on the same block, the wide streets, the unusual architecture and a sun-warmed climate that encourages onlookers in the night hours all make of Wilshire— or K3-45-1, as is called officially—a climb of maximum difficulty at almost every step. My left leg is not well, of that I am sure.

My route travels east to west, my summit to be at the last place possible before the impassable stretch of the Beverly Hills Golf Course, which is the rounded corner of the Bank of Wang Building at the end of the block where Wilshire is crossed by Santa Monica Boulevard. I must therefore enter the route to the east at a point that will make my journey a full thirty thousand lateral feet, or something less than six miles, a feat that neither Gregg, Mitsubi nor Ashton-Whuippy dared contemplate and one which will—once I essay it—effectively close forever our competition with the verticalists, who never scale their full heights anyway since they are invariably carried high up a mountain by some conveyance before they begin to climb and even then can, at best, hope only for the pitiful twenty-nine thousand some feet supplied them by tawdry Everest. No boulevardist has ever achieved anything beyond the twenty thousand and six claimed by Gordon and Singh on their New York City high route (Broadway/M93-02-12) in 1958. Cheated of even this distance in my Chicago attempt, humiliated and jailed, I am left with this smoldering desire to see myself in the top ranks of the sport and of its secret history. The attempt must be made here, now. I am not getting any younger. One more fall or one more day in jail will be the end of me, I am afraid. I have wasted my life in this stupid endeavor. I have nothing, no family, no possessions, nothing. I have no wife, no sweetheart, no companion. I sleep alone. It's now or never.

15TH DAY

Went to a bar on the boulevard last night—the Jungle of Oranges, I think it was called—and met there a woman whose name I never asked. When I left her house this morning I did not know where I was. Even now, I could not find my way back to her. That is all I know. I need more work on my maps. I need to scout more. I do not need futile, meaningless relationships with women whose names I do not know and who do not care if I might ever find them again. I have taken to dreaming. I dream of a woman who will betray me, as Sir Jim Ashton-Whuippy was betrayed. I think I am frightened now, for the first time. Good. It keeps me alert.

18TH DAY

All is ready. The first pitch up will be at the northeast corner of Kanga-roux and Wilshire, sadly the same intersection wherein Gregg and Mit-subi lost their lives in '79 (run over by a catering wagon after a broken rope and fall on their eighteenth side-street crossing). I am nervous and excited but filled with a deadly calm and resolution for what I am about to do. There is a small espresso bar (The Krazy Kup) whose leaded and diamond-paned windows and awning will make my first obstacle. The streetlight at the corner is dim and faceted, however, and will provide a short pull up to the scalloped awning. Next door, St. Ornithal's slick granite edifice can with luck be negotiated by finger-plungers and suck-ers. The adjoining Cochran building is but six stories high, constructed of thick stucco which will accept pitons although the holes will have to be plugged en route. By the first dawn I must be up and concealed again.

I will embark at midnight. Since I have no compatriots to rappel or belay, I must start on the ground, at the corner, in the dead of night, my supplies disguised as a jumble of trash cans and cardboard boxes. I will be unable to wear sharp crampons for fear of puncturing the awning of the Krazy Kup.

19TH DAY

Exhausted, somewhat injured in the leg, but here in Camp One with all my supplies intact and concealed. Initial ascent not without difficulties. There was a woman sitting in the Krazy Kup until well past two in the morning, sipping cup after cup of espresso. Nervous and shaking, I crouched behind a hedge of red trumpet-flowers on Palmetto Street. I could not see her face. She had very long, dark hair. She dawdled, reading some little book, and the waiters kept the place open for her and her alone. They seemed quiet and attentive to her every move. She was entirely absorbed in the book. When she finally left, she lingered a step too long by my supplies, I thought. I was petrified. She was carrying a large purse and I think she wore glasses. Her figure was slim and uncompromising.

21ST DAY

Mostly ten- to twelve-story buildings as I made good speed each night and finally roped and quick-released the crossing at Western Avenue. It is good to be at some height now and I fear the latter stages of the route which drop down to one- and two-story buildings. As I write this, I am aware that I must now enter the world of newer and higher office buildings whose facades dominate many of the blocks ahead and which involve the negotiation of large expanses of plate glass to be traversed quickly, my powdered dry plungers hopefully leaving no marks. I resolve to pay careful attention to the condition of my plunge-locks and above all, prevent the accidental swing of chock or piton, which may shatter the glass. An accident on vertical plate glass is the greatest fear of our fraternity and the results are usually fatal, to which the well-known fate of the Swedish Peterson Brothers team on Indian School

Boulevard in Scottsdale, Arizona attests. Though they fell only two stories, the result was death. The slicing, it is said, was terrible.

I see the deco Dwarft-Western Theatre rising gaudily across Wilshire from my perch. Its decoration comforts me. The last two nights I have traversed a myriad of signs on small and large buildings: Fashion Nails, Nude (monthly) Parking, St. Infirmius Cathedral, something called the Crazy Chicken (I had to mount and traverse the chicken itself, pursued by the random swirlings of the Crazy Chicken Grand Opening spotlight) and then a nightmare block of vacant land bounded only by three-foot-high metal poles along one entire triple-sized city block. This may have been the most difficult thing I have ever done. Spotted by several Homeless, but I think they only saw me as something dark, stringing lines between poles. One of them shouted, "Night spider! Night spider!" but I could not tell if he meant me. It was either the poles or the curb and no one—not even the diminutive Hagworth Smyth-Peggle—has ever successfully negotiated the street-face of that long and low a curb. Finally I am at Crenshaw which I know to be the first mile mark. There is luckily a Mormonic Temple at Lucerne, upon whose mystic dome I will rest for a while.

25TH DAY

The worst thing—of so many bad ones—is this matter of the side-street crossings, because this damned boulevard more often than not enjoys wide intersecting avenues. This makes for generally hellish prospects by contrast with the bigger-blocked cities of the East or the more narrowly side-streeted, tightly-knit cities of Europe and Asia. (Readers may remember in particular, my successful climb in 1977 with the late Sir Jim Ashton-Whuippy of the south face of People's Correction Thoroughfare in Zagreb.) Since one must embrace the entire distance of the designated thoroughfare and cannot merely scuttle the crosswalks like a furtive pedestrian—and if a line cannot be safely and silently flung across—the boulevardist must then find something to actually climb, and automobiles, for better or for worse, are about all there are. (There is a perhaps apocryphal story of one Emmerhelz, a legendary Austrian Streetist of the twenties, who supposedly appropriated the correctly-faced tail-coat of an unsuspecting Vienna burgher during a fierce blizzard and proceeded to scale the man using a bevel sling and two small hook-knouts as the poor chap, twisted sideways by the wind, negotiated through an already fierce storm with this added weight upon his ample back. Not a soul, it was said, saw Emmerhelz as he lifted off and quickly mounted the correct face of an electric transmission pole, leaving one Austrian convinced that the storm had pressed upon him twice the weight of the Devil himself.)

More than I had hoped, I have had to use the oldest and most dangerous technique for side street crossings, the Double Mobile Lentmiere Grade Ascent, first thought to have been formalized by that legendary Frenchman in 1825 on the much slower coaches and horses of that halcyon time. To succeed, this being a country of left-hand drive autos, and my route directed-west, I must first attach myself to the south face of an automobile moving north on the side street—away from the main thoroughfare—and then mount and climb the correct (or headlight) face of an automobile going the other way, back south toward Wilshire. Reaching the corner, with perfect timing, unseen by anyone—most particularly the driver or passenger—I must then make the ascent to the next block before being swept across the boulevard into an illegal maneuver, thus rendering the entire climb a failure. Of course, all this is unknowing if the car will stop or not at the corner. On the Lourdes Avenue crossing which I essayed at four in the morning, two nights ago, there was so little traffic that I was carried clear up to Sunset Boulevard before I found a suitable crossover car moving south. This maneuver is nearly impossible, needless to say, very dangerous and doubly unwise to attempt on the brightly colored sports-cars driven by the kind of blonde woman who seems to abound here. How I escaped being seen by the one I fastened onto at Sunset, I will never know. The top was down on her convertible, but she did not see me as I clung to her grille and headlights and made the step-off to the south face of a "Massive Knockers" magazine dispenser at Wilshire.

(I see them below even now, at five in the morning, the blondes in the convertibles, their hair blowing in the sultry night air, the pigeons scattering before their Corvettes and Mustangs. There is one who drives an open pink Thunderbird in the night, I see her often. She wears dark glasses in the shapes of hearts and she has not looked up at me, not ever.)

26TH DAY

Still set up on the dome of the Temple of Morons, here I can see clear to the sea and what must be Catalingus Island miles out in it. I will sleep here for two nights, if indeed sleep is possible. I am exhausted. I seem secure for now and well hidden because of my construction of a clever nest of plastic twigs high on the golden dome of this old building. It is wonderful to be lofted up here. I have broken out my rip-stop pigeon suit just in case, but so far there have been no watchers in the windows directly across and below in a block of Disney-modern office buildings, each in the shape of a duck or mouse. I look out to the southwest and the end of this stupid endeavor seems terribly far off, unseeable, in fact. I have begun to wonder if all this is worth it, but I remember the words of my mentor, Sir Jim Ashton-Whuippy, and resolve to go on:

"Without secrecy, without furtive endeavor," he told me on his death-bed, "we who haunt these night routes would be nothing. These cities are ours and ours alone and God must have made them for us or he would not have made them at all. If we are lucky, neither He nor anyone else sees us."

28TH DAY

At Runtmore Boulevard, I entered a demanding world of four-story apartments for some blocks where discovery would bring instant disaster. The dark side of our sport most certainly comes into focus here. The essaying of private homes or apartment buildings, at night, can only lead the public to think in terms of so-called "Peeping Toms." I recall the embarrassing moments of the trial of Sir Jim Ashton-Whuippy. I tried to move quickly. I glanced only once through a window and inside I thought I saw the dark-haired woman who was in the Krazy Kup. Is it only coincidence? It is all that I can think. I moved on quickly, for to be discovered there would have been the end of everything. She was dressed in a black silk robe and her TV was set on the educational channel—I thought I discerned elephants or rhinos reflected in the mirrors behind her couch. Her face was hidden. She held a thin martini glass in one hand.

At Resumption Avenue, the mile and a half mark, there was an entire huge block of only low chain-link fence to be scaled. Then there were blocks of modernistic slanting facades and then a school at Aztec Court with yet more chain-link and hedgerow. At Balmoral Avenue I noted passing the two-mile mark, one third of my endeavor thankfully complete. There is only one high building on which to rest here and then my route drops down to one-story structures. At La Brea, the world of beauty seemed to begin in earnest; the "House of One Hundred Percent Human Hair" is right next to the "Happy Times Hair Shop" and the "King of Numbers Beauty Supply" adjoins the Revlon Bank building. Was the woman with glasses in the beauty shop? I swear I thought so. From there to the Miracle Mile Tower and the Korean Bribery Center; to the El King Theatre and the Hunan Snail Winter Garden; and finally I am at my halfway point which falls almost exactly at the famous La Brea Tar Pits. These will comprise my greatest obstacle, I fear.

30TH DAY

The fences and hedges were not easy, and at one point I had to use a sleeping homeless person's north buttock as a foothold. He moaned in his drunken sleep, but did not wake. I strung release lines from a flagpole out across the first stretch of bubbling tar to a life-sized brass mastodon and with the unfortunate full moon upon me, made my way across certain death to it. From this mastodon, then, to another of its elephantine kind standing knee-deep in the stuff. Huge bubbles would surge to the surface and explode beneath me. From somewhere in the vast city I could hear gunshots as I traversed the deadly, sulfurous stuff. From thence I grappled safely, I thought, onto the museum's glass-brick facade.

And then I was discovered. She saw me and I am now unsure if it is for the first time. I will soon be reported, I know. My climb is over. I decided to flee and risk death rather than stay and await arrest. Her face—I have never seen such a one. Alone in the museum at night, she had on glasses that were very thick and a pencil grasped between her lovely teeth and she peered out a little sliver of thick, wavy glass in the facade of the Museum. She was alluring, more beautiful than any woman I have ever seen, lovelier even than the blondes of Wilshire Boulevard in the convertibles of the night. She seemed to glance at me frankly, peering above her glasses. I could not move, suspended as I was some hundred feet above my death in bubbling tar. She dropped her glasses an inch down her nose and leaned closer to the thick slit of a window and observed me curiously. She has very long hair, tied back severely. She wears black. She is the same woman, the one from the Krazy Kup. I have been seen. It is over. Her face was very beautiful. I have always liked a woman in glasses.

31ST DAY

I keep going. Where is she?

During the surprisingly chilly hours between three and five o'clock in the morning, I clawed my way over some really quite interesting marble facing formations not the least of which was a Class Five underslung on a neon sign reading, if I remember correctly, "House of Chez's House." The little plaster buildings interspersed with larger ones along these last few blocks have all been like that, quite the more difficult than they look. Where is she? Was that her sitting in Corky's Coffee Shop at Fairfax with a bagel? Was that her under the dryer at Yamato Beauty College? I am possessed. I fear the worst and hope for the best. Neither, I assume, do I deserve. The nightmarish crossing of San Vicente is my greatest challenge at the four-mile mark. Here there are monstrously wide streets to get across to the Big 5 island and then more to the haven of the ten-story Bank of Singapore building and the official entrance to Beverly Hills. All are restaurants here: Nibblers, the Blue Lobster, the De Lerious Drive-in, the Fertile Egge, Regrets from Rangoon and then at Ribbetson my route drops down to virtually all one-story buildings.

I am at five miles when I reach Doheny. The next sixteen blocks are generally low. I move quickly, expecting arrest. Will she come to see me in jail? The Home Savings Building has in relief a brass statue of father and son embracing in celebration of—presumably—good saving habits. I scale their burnished figures and rappel up the Stock Building and then lash myself onto the windows of the famous talent agency enshrined in the Five-Star/Hopeless Complex, a building shaped like a fish. (It is damnably rounded, like so many of these modern and expensive buildings in this most modern and damnable city.) From Zsa-Zsa Drive west, the streets intersect the great boulevard in a diagonal manner and the side street crossings are necessarily wider. There is Rodeo Drive slanting away. Is that her, threading through traffic with great expensive breads in paper sacks hugged to her slim body? Saks across the boulevard—is that her emerging with bundles of forbidden lingerie? Sotheby's; her at auction? These thirteen blocks are a one-story hell. There is nowhere to hide and the flat roofs are not available to the streetist, of course. Why am I doing this? I disguise myself on the side of Tiffany's. It is a good thing I carried the squirrel suit all this way, I suppose.

46TH DAY

Still here, still roped in, my net hammock swung between two post-Disney structures, each entire building shaped as a dead rabbit and my lines festooned with the useful Christmas wreathing I carry with me. Took a shower in my hammock tonight, the water in the solar bag still quite hot even at four in the morning. I shaved as well, not an easy feat in darkness, in a wet hammock, two hundred feet above the traffic, thinking only of her. I am facing north and looking down too much and sleeping too little. I think of her all the time, every minute. I cannot try any more Two-way Mobile Lentmiere Grade Crossings because of the increase of blondes in convertibles. There seem to be no autos but theirs in the night. They drive up and down the six lanes below. I hear the low burblings of their powerful V-8 engines until the dawn. I am stuck here unless, as I have been thinking, I abandon my summit and return as I came, looking for her.

She is not blonde and she does not drive. She follows me, I know, I hope. Today I saw her in a restaurant—Yogurt Alley—after hours. She was sitting at a table smoking a long cigarette. Her hair hung to her shoulders. Her dress was black and cut low. She had a dark slash of lipstick across her lips. She was reading a book. She looked up and watched me over her glasses with what seemed a little smile as I silently essayed the blue plate glass of the window, one plungered hand or foot-hold at a time. Why does she not betray me? Is she waiting for my summit to betray me?

At night, I am unable to sleep, the broad boulevard below seems filled with the blondes in convertibles, their heads in scarves against the hot wind, their eyes shielded by the darkest of sunglasses.

Salad Days
A Tale of the Old Detective

✧

In talking the other day with my friend, the Old Detective, I expressed the fear that our city would never be the same again, that our old sleepy town—Queen of the Great Basin, Queen of the Angels—was being replaced all too quickly by a multi-cultural metropolitan money-party, its celebrants dancing on a cracked seismic eggshell, pumped up with too much information and too little oxygen. I was surprised to find that it was his opinion that modern Angelenos enjoy a more exciting and romantic town than did the hipsters and molls of what he likes to call his salad days.

"When were those salad days of yours?" I asked idly, knowing that he wasn't exactly busy, that his case load these days was not wearing him down like the cheap heel on a bad shoe. He looked sharply up at me for a second as we shared cups of coffee laced with something stronger.

"Salad days. Oh, I know what you mean," he said and took a deep drag of cigarette smoke down into his hardened lungs. "You must mean those days when someone of your generation feels guilty and fat and figures he should be eating a salad and drinking foreign water out of a bottle."

I said wait a minute, he was the one who had brought it up and after all I didn't think that's what it meant, that wasn't my understanding of the phrase at all. I'd always assumed that salad days were days that came before the main part of the meal, days of inexperience, the prelims of life. But then I had read that the French thought nothing of eating salad at the end of a meal.

"Wrong," said the Old Detective. "Wrong on both counts. That's not what it means, at least not in my case, and Frenchmen do not eat reversed. The Asian peoples eat reversed. From right to left, if you see what I mean."

I only loosely saw what he meant, but he had a look in his eye than made me reach for my notebook.

"No," he said, "my salad days were right here in Hollywood, down on Salad Avenue, which is a one-block dead-end strip of Tinseltown asphalt in between Romaine Avenue and Edith Head Boulevard. I had rented a bungalow from a guy who had once been a big-time forester up in the Hollywood National Forest, which in those days was all that area of the mountains north of Hollywood Boulevard in between Los Feliz and Laurel Canyon Boulevard. This guy's name was Pheasanton and he'd made a fortune by felling all the old-growth timber that used to dominate the upper montane and sub-alpine areas."

"What year are we talking about here?" I interjected quickly.

"My salad days," he said impatiently. "How can you put a date on something as precious as your salad days?" He looked at me directly for the first time in some time and I saw no hint of laughter in his iceberg eyes.

"I believe, if memory serves, that Pheasanton's first name was Abner. If it doesn't, then it might have been Absalom. He was a beefy guy with an edge of sadness to him."

He poured another jigger into my cup. Darkness had fallen over Hollywood, although the temperature seemed higher than when the sun was up. Cicadas buzzed lazily among the orange blossoms in his little courtyard.

"Now this Pheasanton was a fool for a little dame who lived in a log cabin with her father and some goats up where Bronson Canyon is now. Her name was Esther Qwertyuiop."

I stopped him. "The daughter of Edwin Qwertyuiop, the inventor of the typewriter?"

"The very same," he nodded. "About the time Pheasanton showed up on the scene, old Ed passed away in his sleep and so here was little Esther as alone as you could be in a National Forest that was only a few blocks from Hollywood Boulevard. And like I say, this guy Pheasanton was as rich as that Greek that invented the stuff they coat telephone poles with."

"You mean Creosote, King of Thebes?" I said.

"Yeah, that's the guy. Interesting note here, Pheasanton was the guy that felled all those three-hundred-footers up on the old Mulholland Crest Trail."

"Trees that tall up on Mulholland?" I must have sounded incredulous.

"No," glowered the old man. "Telephone poles. They were famous. The British used to come through and mark them as masts for their tall ships but never got around to cutting them."

"Why not?" I asked.

"Who cares? They were busy, I don't know. Anyway, here's Pheasanton sitting on top of the profits of all that and willing to let little Esther be the co-beneficiary, so to speak. And that's when it happened." He stopped and peered at me closely.

"What?" I asked. "What happened?"

"My salad days." He spoke with some triumph. "That's what happened. That's what we're talking about, isn't it?"

I had to admit that it was.

I smiled politely and made little sharpening motions with the tip of my pencil. He leaned forward suddenly and his old oak swivel chair squealed in protest. He softly placed his old feet in their brogans flat on the floor but did not rise. He leaned forward and fixed me with his eyes.

"You see, Esther Qwertyuiop was one of the two woman in my life that I have loved deeply. Esther was like a kind of wood nymph or sprite, you know? She would flit through the autumnal meadows, backlit with the glowing light of the sun or those huge lights they use when they make movies, I forget what you call them. Anyway, she was just beautiful. Porky Samuelson, the picture director, used to say that Esther was like a metaphor in bloom."

"No kidding."

"Nope. No kidding."

Bathed in the sheltering glow of his desk lamp—the one shaped like a fish—I saw the rugged contours of his face soften. Some of the toughness had dropped away.

"I couldn't kid about Esther, " he said. "It's just too painful. even now, months later."

"Wait a minute," I said. "Are you trying to tell me that your salad days were only a few months ago?"

"What do you care?" He stared at me coldly, beginning already to dismiss me. "These are my memories, after all. So just forget it. Get out of here."

I reached the door. I turned and looked back at him.

"Listen," I started in. "I don't mean to be rude. It's just that I so often feel suckered by you, especially conversationally. You're not the easiest person in the world to be friends with."

He stared flatly at me for a moment.

"There's always gotta be some point to a story to make you happy, doesn't there? Sure, okay, Esther said yes to me and no to Pheasanton, but Pheasanton wasn't going to take it lying down, see? He was a big guy and he had a big gun and he also had one of those things with a kind of hook on the end, you know?"

I tried to think. "He didn't have a hand, he had a hook? Is that what you mean?"

"Yeah, except it was worse than a hook. It was a pruning hook. He was a forester, remember?"

"Wouldn't a pruning hook be something that an orchardist might use rather than a forester?" I asked.

"He had a few apricot trees in his back yard," said the Old Detective defensively. "Anyway, who cares. When you're facing a man with a hook that can stab it's bad enough, but his hook could lop off branches up to one inch thick by a kind of spring-operated blade whose tension was controlled by a rope that he held in his good hand. Oh yeah. And there was a pruning saw attached to it, too. Pheasanton had a lot of options in a donnybrook. Not many lumberjacks would tangle with him, I can tell you."

"I thought you said he had a gun."

"Yeah, I did say that. He had the gun in his good hand."

"I thought he had the rope in that hand."

"He had them both in that hand, don't try to trip me up. You can easily hold a rope and a gun in one hand and, like I say, he was a big guy with big hands."

"Uh, huh," I said.

"That's right," he said, with some satisfaction. "Now you're getting the point."

"Which is?" I held my breath.

He looked like a cat who'd just ordered up the Canary Stew.

"Which is, that it's more exciting nowadays here in Hollywood than in my salad days." He looked satisfied with himself for some reason I could not imagine.

"Let me get this straight," I said in the manner of someone who has to get up and go to work pretty early in the morning. "You're telling me that it was not particularly exciting to have a huge, jilted madman coming at you with an unforeseen variety of weapons, crazed with love for Esther Qwertyuiop? That it's somehow more exciting now in the overpopulated, lock-step world of the present?"

I imagined Pheasanton alternately using his gun hand to fire and jerk on the rope as his left swung close to the Old Detective's face with a deadly sawing, hooking or nipping motion.

"What could be more exciting than that?" I said.

He swiveled around in his chair and stood up with a quickness that belied his years. He padded over and opened the screen door to let me out. We stood under the jacaranda, breathing in the blossom-scented night air like two old friends. He put his hand on my shoulder.

"Kid," he said, "there's one thing that's more exciting and that's the big-screen version of that fight. They were shooting it over on the Tri-Bank lot the other day and someone invited me over to watch. Boy, the things they can do nowadays."

"What?" I asked. "What can they do nowadays that's so great?"

He smiled to himself. "Computers," he said. "It's all computers now. Pheasanton looks so real you'd swear he was alive, but it's all computers and puppets and drawings. And smoke. A lot of smoke. One of the prop men said he thinks it's dangerous."

"Pheasanton?"

"No, the smoke. It oughta be banned. There's too much smoke nowadays. But there it is, another thing that's more exciting than in my salad days." He stopped and flicked the butt of his cigarette over the hedge.

Something burst into flame on the other side. He didn't seem to notice.

"You know," he said. "I just thought of something. Salad days might refer to the fact that that's when you're green, like a salad is green, get it?"

I said I got it and with that he nodded to himself and turned back inside without giving me another glance. I wondered, just for a moment, if these were my salad days.

Later, just to make sure, I looked it up. There once was a Salad Avenue in Hollywood, although it was demolished to make way for a video-rental mini-mall three years ago. I decided not to even check and see if something called the Hollywood National Forest ever really existed. I like to think that it did and that the Old Detective won that donnybrook under its spreading treetops and lived happily for at least a couple of weeks with Esther Qwertyuiop. That's the way I like to think things were in our city in the days of wooden airports with green glass windows in their old towers and the red trains chootling right down Santa Monica Boulevard past the banks of wildflowers in the twilight evenings of summers gone by, with the Pacific before them and the palm trees black against the sunsets of the past.

Wolf, the Canine of Canoga, the Imaginary Carnivore. In his brief moments of spare time, he enjoys swooping across the Great Desert in the luminous Green Locomobile. He is afraid of basilisks. He has a jazz beard. He has higher ambitions, but Radio calls him. He likes to hear music behind his voice and he needs it to groove.

Tales of Bebop's Desert

The story of Melchior Diaz is the story of a man killed by a dog, a greyhound to be exact. The year, 1542. Melchior sets off west across the evil desert of death with twenty-five rejects from the army of Coronado (retreating south after the Death of the Moor) to meet up with Alarcon at the gulf of the Colorado. It's winter, so presumably they took advantage of what little water is ever in the Cabeza and reached the Colorado, called the Firebrand. They meet giant Yumans, they presumably cross the great river and get to the Imperial Valley in California before turning around and fleeing East. They come to burning ground, heaving and smoking. A greyhound owned by one of the soldiers chases the herd of sheep that's with them and Melchior, on horseback, at full speed, angrily hurls a lance at the dog. It sticks in the rock-hard caliche desert earth and Melchior goes right into it, the horse being unable to stop in time. The back end of the spear punctures the conquistador bladder and the soldiers, fighting Yumans and probably Seri and maybe O'odhams all the way, carry him for twenty days until he dies.

Or so they said. Did they just kill him and bury him somewhere near our Designer Border and blame it on a dog? Is he still there? Oona often paints the Ajo Mountains when we're camped at Lone Ranger National Monument. One of the odd mountains in this painting is named Diaz Spire. Is the old dead Spaniard still out there?

The greyhound might have made it to Acapulco and his descendants are probably still there, racing probably, wearing tropical shorts and sunglasses and parasailing or some damn thing. Doing the Macarena, probably. Melchior is dust, wherever he lays, far from Spain, out among the Indios.

Bebop and the Lights of Fun

It's RadioNow, nower than even now was a minute or so ago and I am Bebop Loco, baby, the sun-baked early morning man of the big city of lights, the human mirror, the laughing basilisk in the place called Fun-funTown which—let's face it—is not really that much fun.

I am Bebop Loco, my little hoochies, my little cuties, and I watch you from the air and its waves as you drive your lonely car on the twisty roads, avoiding the little red lights as they pile suddenly up in front of you, putting on mascara in your mirror that does not show things in their proper perspective, those things being largely larger than they seem.

I am the radio king of the bun of fun in this city dripping with tortured regret and angry desire. I am Bebop Loco, sweetie, the important voice from the radio waves of FunfunTown, watching the random catchings of the emigrant sweepers too far north of their Designer Border, an osmotic barrier to keep Indians from getting in and to keep terrorists and high-paying American jobs from getting out.

And the big light rises up over us all in the flooding, burning canyons and the big flat bajadas of three-story houses packed together like no one needs to go outdoors ever again. And then the long shadows fall out of the ocean and the light goes and the little reds and yellows burst out of the Funfun towers and the light goes away and I am Bebop Lobo, baby, the night lover, the wolf of darkness.

And all I want is to go home, for my shift to be over, to see my family, my big beautiful big girl and her little girl—our little girl—and to be out of here, away from the changes of formats and gone from the RadioNow tower.

Christmas

So Big Jesus says to Little Jesus one day in a place outside of Ajo on the Res line, he says *Dude, why do we celebrate, on this day of all days, this feast, this eating, this mass, this hunger for companionship and snow? Why?*

And Little Jesus sits back and looks at the sea of longnecks on the table before them and listens for a careful minute to Los Wolves on the juke and thinks to himself that it's nearly December and looks at his brother and says: *Dude, it's because we are the twins with no Father.*

Bullshit, says Big Jesus and towers himself up into a whirling hobobo of a wind of hell and flies halfway down the Alamo Wash and back and sits down and lets the air whirl around him, knocking over several longneck bottles. *Bullshit,* he repeats.

Well, says Little Jesus, *Mom always said so and I'd like to point out in her defense that we didn't see much Fatherly presence when we were kids.*

Every dude in a brown dress in the big white plaster and mud church was called Father, says Big Jesus defensively.

Not the same thing, says Little Brother. *The Electricity was our Father, that's what I think. And like the Hopi dolls and the ones made by O'odhams to look like the Hopi dolls and like the white man with his little Christmas villages with the moving ski feature and adorable snow-covered houses and carolers and so forth and the Zuni guys with the little turquoise animals and all the little bundles and precious things that look like other things and mean something to somebody, the Electricity is good at running through them, whether through wires or mysterious Old People secret methods, and lighting them up literally and figuratively, much like our Father did with Mom the Virgin.*

I don't think that's funny, says Big Jesus. *It's stupid to think of Mom as a model railroad and Dad as electricity.*

I don't mean it to be funny, it's not funny. It's sad to have no father, says Little Jesus.

There is a big pause.

I guess we are each other's father, says one or the other of them, it doesn't matter which.

Bebop: Wolf of Air, Wolf of Night

This is Bebop Loco, baby, on the radio of dreams. I am Bebop Lobo, babysweet, your nighttime messenger of the bad news of the winds of war, of the winds of the deserts of the Other Side of the Tortured Earth. And my baby who is the mother of my baby girl who is the daughter of my baby girl dreams of peace, that her little brother will not die either far from home or at all, that no cars will crash even close to any of her enormous family from Sonora, that no accident will fall upon her child or me.

Or me.

In the little shrine by the Indian Highway across the turquoise desert of the Designer Border between two Ideas, there is the Virgin herself, the woman of clothing, the woman who can probably remember chapter and verse about pieces of cloth she hasn't seen in twenty years, like the Hootchiecutie herself, asleep as I write.

And in the Fresno of my little youth, under the moons of the Sierra, over the black earth of the San Joaquin, war was something your Dad was either in or not in, either Army or Air Force or Navy or Marines; any of whom could lick whomever of whom dared to ask. We bought the houses in rows and we lived the lives of the Spanish of the North, we voted for Ikes and we voted for Jacks and we hoped not to be taken for braceros or wetbacks or whatever our faraway old country relatives were called as they picked the grapes or the almonds or the cottons of the big flat valley.

And war was as far away as a human comedy ever is, near and far, torturing and receding, seething and forgetting. On the radio in the hot nights of summer, the Original Wolf, the man of the border, the Jack you couldn't vote for, rumbled the air and shook the speaker in your old car as you left the Cherry Avenue Speedway and headed for the Air Burger, you told the babe you were with that those old buildings out there by the Airfield, that's where the German prisoners were held, that's the big irrigation ditch that used to have ducks in it when you were a kid, that's Lauck's bakery, where the apple turnovers are as big as whole pies. And war was prisoners and Chinese and Roes, gone as swift as older brothers, gone as bomb drills and commies and the waiting draft. War was all around us, wrapped us up and led our lives, shaped art and shaped words and was the ditch of courage wherein we were still part of our fathers' silent and secret lives. Our war turned out to be the same as Dad's war and this war, Medieval as it may be, is just our same old war.

Speaking Spanish, as we do here above the Designer Border, we will find the poetry of this horrible war. We will find words to surround poison, we will find sleep, we will find the Wolf of Air, pumping life and the news, perhaps, that Annie has had a Baby, that Staggerlee has shot Billy, that there is still something called the Still of the Night.

It's That Time of the Year

This is Bebop Lobo, baby, the Night Howler, the Lonely Lobo, the working all night man. Where is the Queen of the Darkness, the relief babe, the all-night woman who if she came into the station with her secret key could take over and hold down her shift and let me go home to my baby and my little baby? I am Bebop Lobo, you little Hoochie Cuties, not out in my stark green Locomobile, not bouncing up and down on shocks and struts so complicated that you would need to be speaking something other than the Spanish we are speaking now to understand me. I will carve my crazy life on frozen windows of this animal and it will not get much more than ten to the gallon, but it will be so beautiful that the brujos will fade away, will not be seen, will not find the beauty of the skeletons, hopping and bouncing in the great ring of death, hurling each other into polite spectators, so nice compared to the Worldwide Spectacle of Idiocy on the TVs of the Norteños.

I am Radio Bebop of the Respect for Death, of the Sugar Skull, of the little trails and hints and clues, of the respectful wishes that the stupid dead may be bought off and sent back. There is a beauty in this that the Matadors cannot see. The death of a bull is not the death of a man. The Indios are sad for the bull, happy for the man. But a dead man is like a live bull. Get out of his way. Give him little sugar skulls, do not show him pictures of the Dead Man on Two Sticks. Sing him a little song, send him on his way.

If morning were to come, if my shift were ever over, I would to my sleeping women, the big one and the tiny one, past the cactus wrens and the troops of quails and the hyper-intelligent woodpeckers and I would go to sleep as if I had a palatial hole in a saguaro tree without one elf owl in it, drinking beer and keeping me up. It's that time of the year...

Halloween

Every year the Dead would visit him and when they did he would not tell them to go away nor would he welcome them quite. He was polite, offering them what little he had in his cupboard, and he would extend himself for tidbits of conversation. Outside his little house, witches would fly aloft like cardboard blacknesses, brooms tucked tight between their legs. On his porch were orange heads with glowing eyes and jagged teeth and candles guttered in sconces on his sagging walls.

When silences fell upon the little conversations, he would stay still as one does with Native Persons when there is no need to talk and so no one does. We ride in silence, we and the hitch-hikers, in this case Navajo kids from Many Farms or thereabouts. In Navajo Country, the hitch-hiker will not look at you, walks quietly backwards so that when you stop and pull off to the side of the long red road and step out to motion him into your car, he is now looking at you for the first time. You must nearly beg him to ride with you and there is no conversation once inside and traveling. It was that way with him and the visits of the Dead.

When the Dead came visiting, they often wished to dance and drink beer. When the Dead came visiting, they seemed to want to forget, to get a little high, to talk a little loud, to sing a bit. Dead in automobiles would drive slowly by outside his house, the booming thumps of their magnificent sound systems would rumble through the foundations of his little adobe. Their blown V-8 engines purred like panthers, black in the Southern forests. The Dead preferred the big band sounds of El Salvador and the strange northern sounds of Los Tigres and they would park their rigs and join the party. The skulls were not good at showing emotion, but sometimes, as he sat in silence watching the dancers, he thought he could see a little smile here and there.

"I'm hungry for sugar," said the child and her mother said "Quiet, little one. The nice man will feed us soon. He asks for nothing and fears us little and is quiet and unassuming and genteel."

"Still, I am hungry," complained the child. She had travelled a long way from old high-altitude caves where she had been bound in odd positions for some centuries, and her skin had shrunk down on her bones and the tragic story of her former wet and fleshy parts had been at least partially discerned by the producers of at least two semi-scholarly film documentaries commissioned by the Public Broadcasting System.

"We are proud people," whispered her mother. "We will wait for him to offer us sugar."

And when he'd finished showing the big skull with the iron eyes how to plug in the CD player and the other skull thing with the necklace of thighbones had boosted the EQ to emphasize the rock-solid bass players of the South and the beer was flowing, he would motion to the skeletal child and offer her sugar in the form of little heads made of the stuff and other little things, butterflies and crosses and saguaros and woodpeckers, all of delicious sugar. All the Dead would eventually have a bite of sugar somethings, even the ladies with luscious hips and skeleton faces rouged and painted would have a tiny bite, so tiny that it posed no threat to their wonderful figures. The girls in the little skirts and halter tops and high, high heels who danced with each other out by the sulking lowered cars passed sugar from his kitchen each to the other. All the dead would eat and dance and have a beer or two and slide away into the night until finally he was alone.

Bebop at Quitobaquito / The Hootchiecutie at Chaco

All right, I am Bebop Lobo, Baby, child of the great snoring sleeping desert, the crazy puzzle desert that is the only thing beside me, the Bopster, the hilarious and mysterious me—that can cross through the ingenious designer border laid down by Lutherans and Mexicans for reasons known only to themselves and their pitifully shortened histories. I am Bebop, baby, on the radio, hertzing over the Big Sonora at night, the full moon making the Locomobile shine like the devil herself. And I snuggle my hootchiecutie next to me and she is so fine in the green luminous Bopstermobile with the Hilo Desert headers from the Moon and the Flaming Flowmaster Tejano exhaust, the exhaust that sings like the tigers of the North.

And Bebop lays back and snuggles his baby and looks up at the moon and he is the Nightsmoocher, the man of moves, the slow-talking, time-delayed Night Howler.

And she says to me, Honey, let's go home, I bet the kid's still wide awake and I say baby, watch the big desert, watch the Gila Woodpeckers in the Saguaro Hotels, watch the Diamondbacks whether they are smacking the ball or attacking your foot. Watch for a minute and let the big desert sky whirl around you... Your little sister is babysitting and it's just you and the Night Wolf, sweetie and you are a thousand times pretty and she says, you got to work in the morning honey, you've got to go be Bebop Loco, the hilarious man of Mornings so let's go home and

I don't care. Life is good, in this crazy life in the desert where the scorpions glow, where the snorty piglets sleep under the jumping chollas, where the radio plays some crazy Navajo guy and his guitar all the way from Four Corners. Where the Bopper is at peace and the Hootchiecutie loves him. And the night is forever young.

The Money Hat
A Tale of the Old Detective

✪

The Santa Ana winds blew hot and dry as sandpaper and the hills around Hollywood were bursting into flame on a day when I stopped by to see my friend, the Old Detective. He seemed pleased enough to see me, but preoccupied. He sat at his window, a pair of old black binoculars trained on the incendiary hillsides above his bungalow, which sat in the flatter and presumably safer part of town. On his old TV, with the rabbit ears snaking out of the top, I could see the flames shooting out from other fires in other parts of our spreading city. I commented that the firefighters could use a good detective to find out who was setting these blazes, but he said that would take all the fun out of it. I asked him how he could say that.

"You're surprised," he stated flatly. "Sometimes," he said, "detective work is more fun than shooting craps in a barrel. But fun is where you find it. It's a dog eat dog world, sure enough."

I replied that I had always assumed that it was fish you shot a barrel and after a moment he told me that "craps" was a type of fish. I said he must mean crappies, that they were called crappies, not craps.

"Maybe where you come from," he snarled. "In my neighborhood—in my barrel—we called 'em what we damn well wanted to."

He seemed distressed and I realized that he must have been under some strain. Sparks and glowing cinders had begun to drift down from the burnished sky above. The air smelled of fire. I tried to change the subject. He was wearing his usual hat—his detective hat—and I commented upon that fact.

"The money hat, that's what I call it," he said. "People just know you're a detective if you wear a hat like this. You know, it's interesting. No one made a rule that said detectives have to wear fedora hats, they just do. They do it out of habit, I suppose."

I tried to cheer him up. I said that would constitute a hat habit, but he didn't laugh.

"A hat habit would be something a nun would have." He peered through the binoculars up at the hill. "It reminds me of a case I once worked on. It had to do with shooting craps in a barrel, in fact, but mostly it had to do with spiders. And nuns."

I asked him to wait just a moment and he began to roll a cigarette and I got my notebook. I settled in and he took a long drag off the paper tube. The tobacco smelled firm and manly in the charred air. I prodded his memory, told him spiders were a kind of touchy subject with me.

"Well, I agree with you there, little man. In reality, I found out that all spiders want to talk about is flies." He looked old but as healthy as one could hope for one so beaten by life on the streets. His long legs were wrapped up in sheets of some kind and his old slippers slapped on the linoleum with its faded flowers of tropic days gone past.

"Spiders. You can have them," he said. "All they want to talk about is fly futures, fly margins, stockpiling flies, buying and selling flies, transporting flies, breeding and raising flies for profit, slaughtering flies, pricing flies, triple-witching hours of flies, loaning flies, fly rates, borrowing against flies, building equity in flies, governing flies, managing flies, training flies, promoting flies to management positions, self-help for flies, paroling flies, keeping flies from smoking crack, educating flies, keeping flies in their place and—of course—eating flies." He paused for a long moment. "I don't like spiders much," he said.

"Me neither," I said.

"On the other hand, I like nuns. Usually. Let's see...I was working the day watch out of bunco. My partner was Joe Friday, the boss was Captain Adams..."

I stopped him and said that I hoped I was mistaken, but wasn't that the usual opening narration line of an episode of the old television show called *Dragnet*?

"Oh," he said. "Yeah." His face was etched in thought. "I've been watching way too much TV. It's these fires. They're made for TV."

Indeed, sirens were wailing up and down his street and from behind the hill above there welled up a dense cloud of yellowing dangerous smoke. I prodded him, hoping to get the story from him before we had to evacuate.

"Oh, yeah," he said. "Well, years ago, I got a call in my office one day from a guy named Roosevelt Elk who was in some racket out of Montana. Meat, I think. He was pretty well known in this area, high roller, that kind of mug. Big tipper. And this was in the days when you had to have a trailer attached to your car to haul tips around, they'd gotten so big. This was also in the days when cars had rounded up fenders and guys wore hats all day and all night. That's when I got into the habit of wearing the money hat."

My suspicions were on alert. I asked him if this Roosevelt Elk was an actual elk.

"Don't be stupid," he snarled. "How would an elk use the phone? It would get tangled in his antlers, number one; and number two, how would he dial?"

I said that nowadays we didn't dial, we had push-tone phones with numbers that lit up a smoky green color when you touched them.

"Well, in those days the phones had dials that were like submarine hatch covers, they were so big and heavy. It practically took two grown men to dial nine, for instance. People were more self-sufficient then, they didn't cry out as much because you had to have too much help in order to just ask for it."

What about animals, I asked? Were they more self-sufficient then?

"Don't be smart," he replied. "I haven't said that Roosevelt Elk was an actual elk or that the spiders actually talked to the nuns."

"But they did?"

"In a manner of speaking. It was more like a whisper, from what Sister Mortadella told me. It seems the spiders were advising the nuns on investments, the nunnery being pretty flush at that time."

I had him confirm for me that he was in fact talking about the nuns of that famous landmark, the Cathedral of St. Hollywood down in the old section of the town, over on the left bank of the river, under the stately poplar trees. I told him I hadn't known there was a nunnery attached to the grand old edifice.

"Oh, yeah," he replied. "The Order of St. Tallulah, very old, very pious. They supply film to the Industry, grow it right out in that forty acres or so in back of the Seminary."

I told him that I hadn't known that film was an organic product.

"Oh, yeah. Organic as all get out," he replied. "Although it doesn't have sesame seeds on it and isn't labeled Mother Rainbow's Honeynutwheat Krunch or some such foolishness. No, the nuns were doing real good what with the explosion of popular entertainment in those days. They had greenbacks stacked up in the Rectory and had to do something with them, so they did what the spiders told them to do and began to invest heavily."

There was a long pause. I finally said, "In flies?"

He smiled. "Yeah. Exactly. Flies, what else? Especially something called 'Fly Fishing.'"

I said that of course I was familiar with the time-honored technique of using flies to catch fish, but he stopped me.

"No," he said, "you've got that dead wrong. You use fish in order to catch flies. Flies are much harder to catch than fish are. It's more sporting. In point of fact, the way you catch flies is interesting. You attach a fish to a hook and cast it, say with a nine-foot rod on a number three weight-forward floating line with about a twelve foot leader and a one-x tippet, and you let it drift downwind toward a fly, the fly rises, the fish grabs it and bingo, you got one."

"A fly," I said.

"Yeah," he said. "It's a real thrill. We used to fly fish down on the Hollywood river, right by that big oxbow curve where you can see the trumpeter swans, where the elk come down to graze in the evenings."

I said I hadn't known about that place. I hadn't known about the elk and I hadn't known about the swans.

"It was a hotspot in the old days, that's for sure," he said, emitting smoke from his old lungs in huge donut-shapes that drifted above us like flying saucers. Outside, flames were licking at the top of the hill. A line of men in rubber suits dragged big canvas hoses up to meet the blaze. "Guys used to come all the way from Montana to fish that spot," he said.

I asked him if Roosevelt Elk was one of those fishermen.

"Well," he said, "maybe in the beginning. But after awhile this town got to him. By the time I met him, Roosevelt Elk was only interested in smart-talking women with rounded-off heels and hopes of a respectable beauty shop in their cloudy futures, if you see what I mean."

I asked him if he meant women of the night, the lost souls of the boulevard, the queens of display, the girls who live under the moon.

"Yeah, I suppose that's what I mean. But things were tough in those days and you didn't have a lot of picturesque ways of describing things. We just called them floozies. You see, Roosevelt Elk had gotten mixed up with one of them who was saying she was a starlet—and to be fair, she did have a couple of small parts in the movies. She was in *Ring Around the Mattress* for instance and she was in *Roller Maidens from Outer Space* as well. She ran the gamut, if you see what I mean. She had shoulder-length platinum hair and wore those off-the-cuff dresses that were so popular."

I said didn't he mean off-the-shoulder dresses?

"No, these dresses barely had any cuffs at all. They were short dresses, in other words. Get with it. Anyway, seems the nuns reported to the police that someone had stolen everything that had come in from the investments, which was now more than what they'd been trying to get rid of in the first place. The cops fingered Roosevelt for the job, said he was in deep to the Mob. He wanted me to clear him, see?"

"And did you?"

"I tried. He was on the lam. That's a technical detective phrase meaning he was on the run."

I told him thank you and that I was aware of the phrase.

"Well, you never know these days," he said. "The last time I saw him was at the Five Queens, a joint down at the harbor that featured illegal gaming. In fact, that was where they played the game where you shot at

city that had grown up there. The homeless skated by, under the bent palm trees, wheeling silently over the scars of a time in our town when men might have been men and women might have been starlets and dogs might have eaten dogs but when, in fact, spiders called the shots.

We Three Kings of Tacoma Are

✿

The Center Panel

Not too many years past, in that region of the Pacific North where people have settled, wisely or not, around the base of the great volcano Tahoma, and specifically in the misspelled city of Tacoma, in the State of Washington—and on a dark and stormy night—the sodden figure of a drunken man fell to its knees in the humble neighborhood near St. Bart's mighty old dark brick church set high up one of the seven hills above the twisted mystery of the lower Puget Sound. This drunken man on his knees did not pray, but belched hugely and vomited copiously into the welcoming gutter and then he breathed mightily and sat down on the icy curb. It was late in the month of December. He fumbled in his stained garments for a cigarette, the butt of which was found and lit only by using up three old greasy wooden matches. The matches each sputtered blue sparky fire into the Tacoma night.

A lonely car sped by, its tires splashing up a freezing surge of water, spraying this horrible, but by now smoking, man. He solemnly cursed each car that passed, as best he could.

"Fuckin' Cavalier!" he would shout at a Chevy Cavalier. "God damn fuckin' Invicta! Cock-suckin' Toyahto!" and so forth. He gave the finger to each. "Man, ooooh MAN!" he shouted out, for no good reason, in a loud tone of gloom and drunkenness.

Then a little old car passed by, a little old hippie wagon, he thought, but he couldn't quite remember the name for it and so he let it pass. There was a dog inside, he could see, and an old man driving and perhaps the face of a young woman with troubling eyes.

His name was Schrobberbeeck and he was drunk and filthy. He had on clothes, and that's about all you could say about them. He had a beard, did Schrobberbeeck, but it wasn't much of a beard. He sucked grimly on his damaged cigarette and water from his sickened shoulders dripped down into the old brickwork gutter. From inside the dimly lit and secret sanctuary of St. Bart's he could hear the shaky little choir practicing the familiar songs of Christmas. Sad colored lights of the season blinked valiantly, strings of them having been draped over the old church by sober worshipers. The portico leaned at an angle somewhat canted to that of its steeple. The night was dark and darkening yet.

A little thing of light from far away shone down the hill and it came closer and got bigger. It was a flashlight approaching and behind it was Schrobberbeeck's old friend Pat, sloshing up to him in the dark night. Pat (as Pat himself had often enough said) was a large Negro of a man and while he was as poor as was Schrobberbeeck, he was unlike his friend in that he was not a great drinker. He preferred decent marijuana, did Pat, and the twelve-dollar wines of California in what he liked to think of as moderation. Pat's life was marred to a great extent by a mysterious past and he counted himself a tragic figure for reasons never quite revealed to his friend Schrobberbeeck nor to much of anyone else. He walked with a great limp, did Pat, a crippled limp in fact, and he tended to cars for a little living, he washed them and he sometimes parked them and for whatever reason, on this night, he was in a state of transcendent grace and triumph, which was lucky enough given Schrobberbeeck's sad condition of damnation and drunkenness and defeat.

"It is Christmas again, Schrobberbeeck you fucking asshole!" Pat shouted out. "And it is time, my old friend, for the Three Kings to walk! Let them stride out into the heart of this dark and Holy Night! Is this not true? This night, this holy night, set aside for the celebration of the birth of Our Lord! In this land! Even here high above the mighty fucking Puyallup River!"

Pat's words rang out into the freezing night. As if in response, somewhere down in Tacoma, a Harley-Davidson motorcycle roared to life. Frigid shafts of milky light struck down through shattered little clouds. The iced moon shone out briefly and then was gone.

Schrobberbeeck hiccupped gamely. He vomited again, a small but virulent vomit.

"Lord, but it smells like Hell itself out here, Schrobberbeeck, old son! God himself would be proud of such a stink!" And Pat hoisted his drunken friend up onto feelingless feet and so propelled him into some ceremonial and hopefully useful action. He had to do this pretty much every year because he needed money every year, and so needed Schrobberbeeck, however drunken his condition. Besides, it was exactly the season of forgiveness and of drunkenness.

He needed Schrobberbeeck on every blessed Christmas when he and Schrobberbeeck and their friend Crab Man would then, upon his urging, carefully remove the sacred symbols of their kingship from the secret places where they had been hidden all the year long, mostly tucked away in the rafters of Schrobberbeeck's sagging garage on the alley in back of his downtrodden little house on Alder Street. These holy symbols were hidden there because Schrobberbeeck was the only one of the Three Kings who actually lived in a house, such as it was, and had therefore a garage, such as it was, and therefore a fit place in which to hide things away.

In the blessed season, the three of them would find up there the marvelous silver star of heavy-duty aluminum foil atop its long telescoping aluminum pole, once a fixture of some North End swimming pool; they would produce again their cardboard crowns and swords, wrapped in regular-strength aluminum foil by innocent third-graders at the Longfellow school and stolen from them with no regret; they would carefully lift out the manger, cleverly fashioned from a supermarket cart never returned to the Thriftway market, filled with glittery paper for straw and, as in every year, Pat would not have to blacken his face in order to portray the Dark King. The joke was as good this year as it was every year and, as in every year, the Crab Man and Pat laughed, although Schrobberbeeck, being too drunk on this night, did not.

Crab Man was so-called because he eked out a smallish living selling crabs to idiots and tourists down on Ruston Way, lurching from bicyclist to roller blader with a portable tray full of evil-smelling old dead crabs on not much ice. He worked out of the back of an ancient GMC Suburban decked usually with signs reading: "Crabs, One Dollar. Fretch Shrimp." Crab Man was as stubborn and secretive and clever and sideways as a crab and pretty much a confirmed smoker of cocaine, although he did not exactly admit to it. He needed money, for whatever reason, and more than once had resorted to easy burglaries in neighborhoods accessible to his ancient vehicle, or so the police of Tacoma will be happy to tell you. He had long stringy hair and a devilish moustache and beard and he was one of those people whose frayed jeans seemed to cut across worn-in old high-heeled cowboy boots at exactly the right place. Crab Man was known to be attractive to certain women of the town, in other words, and that made of his life a living hell, as he was quick to point out to his two best friends, who, if he had to name them, would have been Pat and Schrobberbeeck. For the most part, Crab Man lived in Schrobberbeeck's decrepit front room on a couch whose springs had seen one or two many thumps from one or two many rumps. When he needed to deal seriously with the annoying women of the town, he would take them to the trailer he theoretically owned, the old aluminum one parked down by the Puyallup River, under tall alder trees filled with roosting crows, because he was technically an Indian and the river land was Reservation Land. He was only about a quarter Puyallup, but that was more than enough, as he often said, certainly more than once.

It turned icy cold and crisp and finally began to snow on the Christmas night that these Three Kings, decked in their sacred symbols and pushing their manger on supermarket wheels, set out to sing their Christmas carols in this year in the city of Tacoma, which is a place of temperate enough climate—with albeit much rain—that snow is almost always a novelty. For it to snow—good snow, snow that stuck— could be counted almost a miracle in this place and especially on this night.

The three sad figures, after some years of practice, could sing "Silent Night" pretty well. They could sing "We Three Kings of Orient Are," both the versions sacred and profane. They could sing "Adeste Fidelis," although they had not one idea between the three of them of what any of it meant. They made quite a sight in the slump of thick snow that fell over Tacoma at rush hour, in the darkened night. They wore fake beards and robes that held many patterns popular with bathrobe makers and their great silver star glinted brightly above them when Pat twirled it on its long pole. It was more snow than Tacoma may have ever seen and it came down slowly, without wind or storm. It came down for hours that night. It snowed and then, amazingly, it snowed some more.

And these were flush times for Tacomans, the year had been a prosperous one and the goods and services, the fish and lumber, the cameras and carwashes, the meats and the motors and the glassware, the everything and the everything else had all done pretty well and the fattened people of the town sat before their glowing TVs and contemplated at least this one Christmas without need.

Not only pedestrians but slowing cars gave money to the Three Kings this year in amounts they had never before imagined. For a while they stood amazed on the corner of Division and Tacoma and sang "Jingle Bells" at the top of their lungs, but the traffic was piling up to see them and give them money and so—at the polite request of Sergeant Ng of the Tacoma Police—they moved down onto Pacific Avenue, that important boulevard, under the gentle wash of an amber streetlight that bathed them with what could have been a holy light, the way it cut neatly down through the falling snow. There, too, people seemed eager to give them money. They were wished "Merry Christmas" time and time again, and they would shout it back with the good cheer that naturally comes as coins and bills pile up in your manger, making it so heavy that it could not be wheeled, but had to be dragged from place to place. They drank from bottles concealed in their robes and Crab Man left briefly at about nine-thirty and returned with a gram of cocaine that kept each King awake and alert, singing and full of cheer.

It was almost midnight, certainly quitting time for the Three Kings, and Schrobberbeeck could barely refrain from counting all the coins and bills right then and there when a big dark stretch limousine pulled up, its many tires crunching in the snow, and a rear door opened and a voice issued out. It was the voice of a man, a deep-voiced man. He had long hair dyed three colors down to his waist and was wearing an expensive black three-piece suit of elaborate design. Half of his head was shaved and dyed a purplish color. His shirt was open and necklaces were draped around his throat. His fingers were studded with rings that flashed fire brighter than Schrobberbeeck's wooden matches into the night. On his feet were high-heeled boots covered with the skins of animals never before seen in Tacoma and which Pat immediately thought were worth more than he on the open market. Pat was not on the open market, which was the way he put it, ever aware of his troubled ancestry.

"I am an Enslaved-American, not an African-American. I am a child and grandchild and great-grandchild of the survivors of slavery. We are adapted to slavery as naturally as a woodpecker is adapted to pecking wood. And here we are, genetically ready to please, in a country full of motherfuckers comically dead set against what they seemed to be absolutely committed to a hundred and fifty years ago, to the point that this very nation would not have been worth fighting over were it not for our Enslaved Negro labors." This was the way Pat talked when he had some decent marijuana and a bottle or two of Pinot Noir from the Napa Valley. (If Schrobberbeeck joined him in smoking marijuana, after a pause, he would ask if the woodpeckers were absolutely committed as well and after a decent pause, Pat would just laugh like hell.)

"You've got a point, Mr. Man," said the Rock-and-Roll Person from Seattle, after Pat had regaled him with something close to his usual Enslaved-American speech. "We're free tonight because of you. What's your name?"

"I am the Dark King," said Pat with some dignity.

"Well, here, Kings of Men, have a cigar or three," said the man, offering them several expensive-looking cigars in his bejeweled hand. "And a Merry Christmas to you."

"That is not a rubber cigar, is it?" asked Schrobberbeeck suspiciously.

"No, it isn't, not at all," the tall man laughed, his little eyes twinkling against the velvet of the luxurious velvet seats. "It's a damn illegal Cuban cigar, my friend," he said. The exhaust of the limo billowed out, as if any more of a theatrical effect were needed; the three Kings next to the long black limo in the snow, lit from above by a great shaft of amber streetlight flickering down through the fall of unusual snow-flakes.

"Let's hear you boys sing it, though," said the great man in the great car.

The Three Kings looked one each at another and smoked at their cigars and then dutifully sang the profane version, hoping for more largesse from this strange man. To be sure, they weren't exactly sure of all the lyrics. They sang:

"We three kings of Orient are,
Tried to smoke a rubber cigar.
Something, something…
It expl-o-o-ded…
Now we're something…
Something something."

"Well, that's close enough," said the Rock-and-Roll man meditatively. He reached back in the limo and pulled out a little leather bag, heavy with some important weight.

"Merry Christmas, you three idiotic kings," said the man, sadly.

"She doesn't want to see me." He stared straight for a moment and then he said, "So I'm going back to Seattle." The door closed and the great white limousine plowed into the fresh snow in the street, leaving four snakes of blackened tracks twisting off into the holy night.

When the Three Kings looked into the leather bag, they found money, both in bills and some coins, some rare coins as well, some little gold and silver bars and several rings and a necklace worth perhaps some thousands of dollars, thought Crab Man, who did not mention that fact to the others. Still, it was a lot of worth. Schrobberbeeck produced a wooden match. It sputtered blue fire into the night and three cigars were re-lit. They were rich, although Crab Man hoped to be richer.

They headed for the American Wigeon Tavern on Broadway. They would get drunk there and eat prime rib sandwiches with au jus and horseradish, they shouted, but instead, they got lost in snow so heavy they could not find their way in their own city. Christmas seemed far away, the snowfall was so great. Tacoma itself seemed far away. The wind picked up and began to howl and the snow began to drift and there were no cars or passersby on the whiteout streets of the town. They pushed their shopping cart in vain, its straw falling out on the snow. They contemplated automobile theft. The streetlights went out, as did all the lights in town, one by one. The streets were deep in snow. They did not know where they were or where they had come from. For a while, they thought they saw light coming from the gutters of the snow-buried streets. From there, from beneath, they heard a great sound like the magnificent humming of more bees than anyone might ever imagine.

They tried the handles of the doors of cars left foolishly on the unfamiliar streets. They came upon a kind of hippie wagon on Yakima, near Division and the Frisko Freeze. Its little lights shone out into the night. When they tried the door, it was locked, but inside the car they could see that in the back seat there was a woman and a newborn baby who had been wrapped in a leather jacket with a skull embroidered upon it.

The woman and her new baby were set out comfortably enough. The car's heater had once been working and the interior must have been just warm and the Holy Spirit itself seemed to smile right up at them as they stared through the frozen windshield. A large golden dog laid with its head upon the woman's lap, the baby beside. The old man tried once more to start the car.

"One more step and I'll shoot you with the gun I have," shouted the old man at them, but the engine refused to turn over. The Three Kings looked so funny in their stupid tinfoil crowns that the woman laughed in spite of herself. "You won't do us harm," she said, in a firm manner. "But if you don't help us, my baby will freeze solid."

"Don't you have anywhere to go?" yelled Pat, scraping ice away and tapping on the window.

"We have nowhere to go and we have nothing to eat," shouted the old man. "Ho, ho, ho."

"Well, you can't let her stay out here," shouted Pat.

"Go away," the old man yelled.

"We came to ask you the way," shouted Schrobberbeeck, suddenly inspired from he knew not where.

"This is the way," called the Old Man, simply. "Come in," he said to them, making sure they saw his lips move. The doors became unlocked then.

There was a big yellow dog in the car. The woman wore a blue robe with a hood and the old dog lay its head on her knee as she nursed her little child. The little child laughed at them, through his suckling. Schrobberbeeck knelt down in the snow, suddenly, not really knowing why he did and so did Pat.

The old man tried to start the car. The little engine turned but did not turn over. "It's no use," the old man said. "Out of juice. We have no money."

"What do you eat then?"

"We have nothing to eat."

The three Kings looked at one another and then, without even consulting each the other, they gave the old man and the woman and the smiling suckling child everything they had, including the bag the strange rock and roll man had given them. The woman smiled gently.

"God will reward you," said the old man. "Ho, ho, ho," he said, most gently.

The Kings trudged home through the freezing snow.

"Couldn't the child have been God himself?" asked Schrobberbeeck.

"Don't be stupid," said Crab Man. "God has good cars and can clothe himself, even as a child he could."

"But he was born poor, in a stable, in a manger—whatever that is. I don't think it was in a supermarket cart."

"But that was long ago."

There was a long pause in the freezing cold. "Why, then, did we give them everything?"

"I wish I knew. I wish I knew."

They found the bar and inside the patrons laughed and sang. They stood outside, with nothing to their names.

The Second Panel

Again, the next year, it was Christmas. Pat was very ill, laid out, sick in bed at the motel opposite the Pick-Quick Drive-in out on the great road across from the willows by the creek along the road that serviced the great docks of Tacoma. His two friends had gone out without him and yet they sang that they were the Three Kings. He lay in his bed and thought feverishly about the last year when they found the woman and the child and the golden dog and the old man in the hippie wagon and had given them everything they had been given.

Pat now felt certain that the little person had been God himself. Since that time, Pat had become a different man. Here is the way, the old man had said. His two friends, Schrobberbeeck and the Crab Man seemed to have already forgotten the incident. "How strange, how strange," they would say, but he could tell they didn't even really remember.

But Pat had changed his life. He knelt before the statues. He followed after them, he went on the rounds, he forgot his tending of cars. He sang pious songs and tried to atone for his previous sins. He began to freeze himself and hurt himself for reasons of crazed piety. His leg dragged. He spoke to people about sin, now, something he would formerly have laughed at. People at St. Bart's thought he had gone crazy.

He had been longing and looking forward to this Christmas. He kept the star and he made it better. He told his friends he would only go with them if they would give their earnings to the poor, of which there were still too many in Tacoma.

"We are poor enough for all of them," said Schrobberbeeck firmly.

"Any idiot can make a star," said the Crab Man.

Pat kept the star, with which they found God last year. He would not let them take it.

Pat was dying. Now death came to him. He could see the star, propped up above the clock radio that glowed greenly in the night, playing out its scratchy carols. The moon came out and climbed up the sky. Pat prayed for one more night of life.

He climbed out of the motel bed and fell and rose. He grasped the star and turned it toward the holy moon and he sang:

"We Three Kings of our star are
We have come here from places afar.
We went and searched and searched and failed
We went and searched o'er hill and dale
And there this star stood still
And there we entered with good will"

He cried and cried and turned the star. The child came to him through the snow although it was only rain. The child had a map of the world and an old pencil and a sweatshirt that said Seahawks on it. He was sweet and Pat recognized him at once.

"I have seen this child before," he murmured. His motel room was filled with the smell of daffodils, although it was far from their season.

"Hello, Pat," said the little child. "I have come to you since you can no longer come to me. Sing your song again. Sing the part, though, about the exploding cigar. It cracks me up."

As Pat sang, an apple tree outside burst into flower in the night, as if it had snowed indeed.

"Come with me," said the little lad. "We have a house now, and a carport and you must come with me." Pat went with him and the golden dog followed behind. He saw spring in the Puyallup Valley and the crocuses and daffodils were in full flower in the driving and freezing rain of winter on the dark tide flats.

"How beautiful it is," said Pat and he died.

When Schrobberbeeck and Crab Man came back to look in on him with some guilt, they had collected only enough coins and bills to have gone to the tavern and drunk and they were as drunk as Two Kings might be, but their pockets were empty. They looked in the window and Pat was dead.

When they opened the door to the motel room, it smelled inside strongly of flowers, as if it were spring too early.

The Third Panel

In the next year Schrobberbeeck became fearful. He was afraid, or so he said, of God himself. He was frightened of Christmas, though, and that was the truth of it. It was Pat's death, in that last year without snow, that did him in. Now he went to church every day. He was not of the faith, but he went to St. Bart's every day. He feared truly the coming of Christmas. He missed his dead friend Pat and he missed the Crab Man, for that guy could make him laugh like no one else, but his fear kept him in his old shack. His car died there and he never left except to go to St. Bart's or to Wright's Park where he would look at the statues, many of whom, he said, had begun to speak to him. And he would venture out at night to steal.

Crab Man now associated with the devil himself. He had got a job hauling equipment for a metal band and so he was rich and it was said that he worshiped Satan. He was the one who said this, actually. He told a story of crabbing, the wind whipping up a hundred-year storm and taking his clothes away and in this naked state he was blown upon a Satanist in Mason County, where such things are said to be common, and the Satanist, thinking he was the Devil himself, taught him the workings of the book of the Devil. The book was called the Black Ambrosius. He would not crab at night, in fact he would not leave his trailer at night. And he and Schrobberbeeck drew apart and did not see one another. It was said that he was rich and he was not the only one who said it.

Schrobberbeeck was drunk, however, this did not change. And he stole. This did not change. This Christmas, as in the one two years ago when they had seen the child, it snowed like a miracle. He feared Christmas, afraid of some holiness, some awful miracle. The snow piled up and up, the moon was full and night was still and the stars were out in the black-blue sky above. He had decided to walk to midnight mass, in order that the Church might ward off the mystery. He did not take the star this night.

He set out clutching a flashlight although the moon was so full and bright the light was not needed at all. The bell called out in the thick white night. He was frightened. Not another soul was out. He cut through the park. The Christmas night wanted something from him.

Frightened as he was, he looked for the statues in the snow, the deep snow. These were his friends now, the statue of Nietzsche, the statue of Puget, the Mother of Christ, the statue of Vancouver, the statue of Ole Olafson, the statue of Babe (the Blue Ox), the statue of the Unidentified Man, the statue of Mrs. McPherson, the statue of the Spirit of the Pacific, the statue of the Dead of the Great War, and as well all the little weeping statues in the roadside shrines for the accidental dead crushed by automobiles or fortune. But where were they on this night? All gone, every one. He froze with terror.

He saw a little figure running through the snow. A little woman, weeping. He had seen her before, on her pedestal, she might have been Jane Austen, she might have been Our Lady of the Seven Sorrows, she might have been the Spirit of Temperance or the Spirit of Pacificness.

But he ran to the Woman of Absolution, he ran to the Mother of the Christ. Seven tin swords were driven through her heart.

"Dude," she said, looking up at him, panting for breath.

"Dude. You've got to carry me! I'm exhausted because I am too small to negotiate my way on foot through the depths of this snow. If I were to acquire a little hippie wagon or even a mini-van I wouldn't need your help, if I could afford the gas and if my feet could reach the pedals. But I know you, I've seen you, you must help me. Carry me, Mr. Schrobberbeeck."

The bell tolled too many notes through the thick white night.

"Holy Mother I cannot pick you up," he cried out in fear and trembling, awaiting the mystery, awaiting his end.

"Listen, pal," she said shortly. "I must make it to my son's mass at the Pond, his big Christmas party and I will be late because I was made late. This evening, as I was preparing to attend my Son's feast—plenty of time to get there even in this stupid snow—a pitiful man came to me, to pray to me. He was a fisherman, he said, and had fallen in with a defrocked priest who had taught him the ins and outs of the Black Ambrosius. He prayed for my help and he was so piteous that I stayed to help him."

"He is saved then?"

"Yes. Hurry, carry me now."

His heart rose and his care dropped away and he picked her up and ran with her, light as a feather, through the beautiful snow.

His steps seemed to sail, to fly. Over a long stretch of slope and snow, he saw a moving cross, dimly seen, heading a little parade that struggled up the hill through the park and toward who knows what. It was an unholy parade, perhaps, but he stopped for breath he did not know he had and he could see around the procession, the statues in human form gathered around the central float and up upon it was certainly God himself, so far as he knew.

"Put me down," she said. "I will not be late for my son's feast." She looked back at him.

"Forgive me," she said enigmatically, her tiny self then turning and trudging through the snow. A small music, something about reindeers perhaps, drifted up to him from the parade.

He could not go on without seeing something, he thought, although he was clearly not invited. He crouched behind a tree and stared. He saw all the statues, but in their human forms, all gathered around the windblown float that came up last in the parade, upon it a great figure of a man, bearded with age, clothed all in red and white. The littlest Mother stood up next to the saint, whose large being graced that float. His heart was as big as the storm that had been. Around the figure were all his mothers, not as solid statues, but as living things: The Mother of Five Wounds, the Mother of Imaginary Reindeer, the Mother of Red Roses, the Mother of Daily Bread, the Mother of Refuge, the Mother for a Holy Death, the Mother of Ho Ho Ho, the Mother of Devotion, the Mother of the Woods, the Mother of Seven Sorrows, the Mother of Jolly, the Mother of Rest, the Mother of Lovers, of Purgatory, of Invention, of Giving. As Schrobberbeeck watched, from far away, he saw that Santa's heart might burst like a grape the way he'd heard Christ's had. He shouted out then, a shout as loud as that he'd shouted at cars but two short years ago.

He shouted out "Hey!" And then, "He is forgiven!"

All the heads of all the paraders snapped around but they could not see Schrobberbeeck, hidden as he was behind a tree, and the float lurched forward somewhat, drawn by a small lawn tractor, and then suddenly there was a loud crack and the ice broke on the Pond where they all stood and the ice was thin and covered with snow so they had not known the danger when they paraded and then the float tipped perilously and Santa was thrown off, clutching at tinsel and everyone ran out in a circle from the sinking tractor and float. Ice cracked, music drowned, little screams and shouts echoed up the slope. Santa's heart, so far as Schrobberbeeck could see, did not break.

Why this made him happy, he did not know. But he was content and went on to Mass and prayed and knew not why. He made his way the long way around. Snowplows had begun their work. He slept peacefully, not so drunk after all.

The next day all the statues were back in their places, made of their familiar materials, far from being human flesh. A groundskeeping crew—after hauling the float out of the pond—found Crab Man, his hands grasping at the bars of the black iron grate that enclosed the little Lady of the Seven Sorrows. A yellow snake lay beside him with its belly slit open, terrible to behold. Crab Man was as dead as the Dead Ambrosius himself.

Schrobberbeeck became a different person. He lost all fear and await-
ed solemn moments. He longed for more mysteries. He looked out for
them and they were his friends. Outwardly he seemed the same. He
lived in his horrible broken house on Alder Street and he drank and he
stole. These things were in his bones and not even the strongest emotion of his soul could change that about himself.

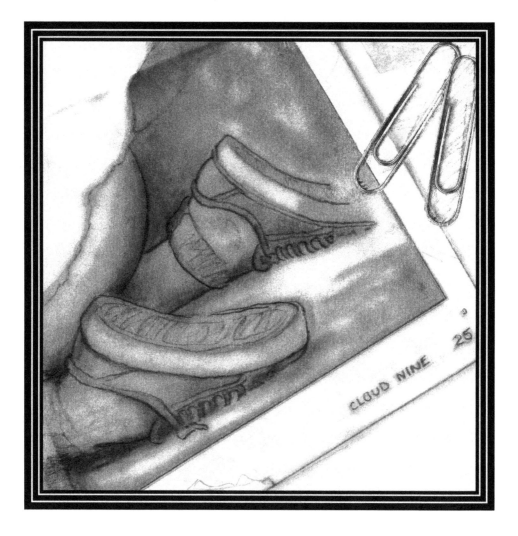

The House of Little Men
or, The Futile Attempts By Men To Control Women

✿

When he was very much younger than he is today, in the beautiful and mysterious city of San Francisco, two women—a brunette one and a blonde one—were momentarily kind to Ballinger at a time when he needed kindnesses of one sort or another for the shaping of a life which had but barely commenced and which was not without considerable confusion, as is the case with most young lives. In this city of San Francisco, because of these real women, enough happened—although it seemed very little at the time—to produce the first chiseling-away at the rough marble of a life among women that, years later, would come to him to seem like not such a bad life at all.

Ballinger was barely twenty in those days, the now obscured and nearly forgotten early 1960's. He had gone away from the town and family in which he had grown. He had been lucky enough to find barely affordable lodgings in a big old comfortable Victorian house overlooking California Street, just below the quiet and wealthy charm of Pacific Heights and just above the noisy bustle of the burgeoning district around Steiner Street which was colorful but not exactly flush with cash.

In this improved place (that is, it was not out in the great flat maligned San Joaquin Valley of central California), he had set himself a superior distance from his country home. The life of the city boiled around him. The traffic, more than he had ever seen, whizzed in double file up and down the terrifyingly steep hills. Towers and castles hung from the sheer rocks. He could hear, from his window, the faint singings of a Baptist choir which was unfortunately seldom in tune and which seemed, regardless of the members' colors (they were, like the City itself, mixed), to be devoid of what was then just beginning to be called soul. Still, Ballinger had thought to himself, still, this was just fine. He could hear the clanging of the antique bells on the cable cars as they clattered up California Street toward the great palace hotels of the town. In what he came to call the House of Little Men, he had the entire front half of the third story above the garage.

The House of Little Men itself was a comfortable old place that might have been a faraway model for the sheltering domicile that Louisa May Alcott depicted so vividly in her book called *Little Men*. Like that nineteenth-century New England nest, it was filled with an odd collection of male humans who, like orphaned boys, lived with each other and all too often only for each other, because there were no real women in their pathetic and lonely lives. In Alcott's story, there presides over the orphans the dear woman called Jo, who is mother to them all. In San Francisco, in the House of Little Men, confronted by Spook, in Ballinger's early life, there were two women: the Blonde Bombshell, who was not motherly at all but entirely mystical, and the Dark Actress, who, while earnest and wild, was full of only conventional wisdom.

Ballinger's apartment in the House of Little Men consisted of what must have been, in earlier days, a large dining room with an alcove for serving. In this alcove, behind screens, he slept, finally far away from colleges and families, alone at last, a young man with two jobs and the world ahead of him. His housemates—the orphaned boys—were primarily Japanese nationals, young men who had been assigned to the newly established San Francisco office of the venerable firm called Japan Airlines. In fact, that was how he had come to live in this place, because he had found a paying job, working nights for Japan Airlines down on Union Square. It was a good job, because it allowed him to continue being an actor of sorts in the play *King Lear* by William Shakespeare, wherein he played many small parts over the course of an evening as a very junior and unpaid member of a prestigious company inhabiting a dark old theatre down on Geary Street.

Ballinger was at an age where the dilemmas of King Lear were beginning to make some sense to him. Not the dilemma of age, certainly, but the problems of a man's relations with women. King Lear's problems, although they are legion, seemed to Ballinger—when you boiled everything down—to amount to only one thing; King Lear runs afoul of trying to control women. The fact that the women in question are his daughters was neither here nor there, to Ballinger's way of thinking. Women were women when it came to problems. In this particular production of *King Lear*, the youngest of Lear's daughters was played by the Dark Actress, a lovely woman who was destined to eventually become the star of a movie so important that it would come to be beloved by his entire generation, in fact it would come to largely represent that generation as it cut its huge swath through time and America. She was, of course, as beautiful as actresses must be and she was young, as actresses must once be, and she was haughty and down-to-earth at the same time. She was the daughter of Lear's dreams. She was everything confusing and wonderful in Ballinger's dreams.

Ballinger's job in *King Lear* was mostly to stand behind the real actors, dressed in wrappings of burlap, holding a barbaric, tattered banner or huge beaten sword while looking at least interested, if not horrified, at whatever nightmare of insanity or cruelty or blindness was being played out in front of him. He had one small speaking scene in which his one or two lines seemed to be some ancient joke known only to Shakespeare and three or four Elizabethan lawyers who by now would be about four hundred years old. The sentiment was clear, however. Once you've stood by and watched the people you work for put out an innocent old man's eyes, it behooves you to make a couple of interesting literary allusions and vow to go and get a crazy person to help lead the old man around. It wasn't much of a scene, but in those days, Ballinger thought he wanted to be an actor and this seemed an excellent way to start. Acting, it turned out, was not for him because, as he thought later, he was a person most suited for a profession that encouraged scattered thoughts—a writer, for instance, or a scientist, or a clown—but he nevertheless did learn something very important, which was that the most beautiful and desirable woman he had ever met up to that time was not in the least interested in him. The Dark Actress, a quiet girl with great liquid eyes, roamed around his brain at all times, which included his lonely stints in the nearly-empty all-night offices of Japan Airlines, where he would talk haltingly on the phone in rudimentary Japanese to elderly people who wanted to make reservations in order to fly back to the old country.

When, in the mornings, he would pilot his green-and-white Buick convertible with the silver portholes plunged into its fenders home through the fog to the House of Little Men, there would be no one around for the most part. But in some unseen room on some floor toward the back, there lurked a huge, misshapen Caucasian thing; male, retarded and voluble, of some indeterminate age. It had a name, presumably, but to all in the house it was known only as Spook.

Spook was not a recluse. He was friendly to a fault, the fault being invariably one of aggression. Ballinger was an unwilling captive in a conversation with Spook, and so tried to avoid them, especially when Spook was holding a chainsaw, which he often did in the early mornings when Ballinger had got off work and settled in for his lonely dinner/breakfast of hash browns and eggs in preparation for going to bed in broad daylight (which, it being San Francisco, was a state seldom observed). His daylight hours were precious to him and many of them came, unfortunately, in the peak hours that Spook roamed and talked and gesticulated inside the House of Little Men.

Spook, on these occasions, would hover cheerfully in the kitchen, brandishing his chainsaw and often firing it up just so that Ballinger could get the full point of why he had a chainsaw, which was chiefly the fearsome damage it might do. Spook, it seemed, had enemies. Chief among them were the Russians, in those days a faceless mass of communists with ill-defined but nevertheless evil intentions. They were about to find out that Spook was plotting trajectories for the rockets of the United States as well as theirs. These trips to Russia to plot trajectories were secret affairs, usually lasting a weekend.

"So," Ballinger would say nervously. "So. What did you do over the weekend, big guy?"

"It's a secret," Spook would say. "I've been in Russia, planning trajectories for their space rockets."

"Ah," Ballinger would say. "Ah."

Then Spook would rip the pull-cord of the chainsaw and it would leap into hellish action, screaming with rage, spewing droplets of oil, reeking of gasoline and whirling its little blades in a rattly racket as if vertebrae were racing up and down some steel backbone within the confines of the little yellow kitchen with its Victorian moldings and its old gas stove.

"THAT'S WHY I'VE GOT THIS," he'd shout over the ratchety roar.

Spook, upon questioning by Ballinger, would admit that there was a kind of ill-defined master plan in these secret trips to Russia. Over the years, as he thought about Spook's scheme, Ballinger would come to see some deeper meaning than just the foolishness it at first seemed. The scheme was this; the world, Spook told him, was controlled by women (this was something that Ballinger was old enough to be aware of), but, Spook pointed out, women were controlled by the moon, that was well known. (Ballinger did not know if this was technically true; but given his obscured knowledge of women, he certainly thought it had some merit as an idea. It seemed positively Shakespearean, in fact.)

"Ergo," said Spook (although that was perhaps not the exact word he used), "control the moon and you will control women. Control women and you will control the affairs of men. Control the affairs of men and you will effectively control the world."

There was a graceful elegance to this argument that seemed unassailable then, although in later years it came to seem quite assailable. Still, it retained for Ballinger, over his long life, an ineffable air of wisdom and mystery.

To give an idea of how limited were Ballinger's perceptions of women, there was, down a steep couple of blocks from the House of Little Men, a grocery store which carried a good selection of Chinese produce and foodstuffs—dark green, glistening twisted beans, mysterious wet vegetables, noodles and petrified red ducks. These things were laid out next to a rack of the rather modest girlie magazines of the day of which one in particular sticks in his memory even now. This magazine was called *Cloud Nine* and when he shyly leafed through it, in lieu of buying food, he saw that it contained page after page of pleasant and naked and smiling young women, most dressed only in low white tennis shoes, each topped with the then-currently fashionable helmet-headed bouffant look to their hair-sprayed hair. These women seemed to enjoy displaying themselves and their nakedness for unseen photographers. Cloud Nine was a peppy world, or so it seemed, probably because of the tennis shoes, which gave a kind of sporting look to every activity of sexual display. He had often heard the expression "Up on cloud nine," but he had given it no special meaning, thinking of it only as an imaginary place like "Easy Street," perhaps, and neither Easy Street nor Cloud Nine had seemed to him to be the domain of peppy fecundity, romping-grounds of naked young women with helmet-heads of careful hair. In later years, when he heard the expression, he knew precisely why a person was happy on Cloud Nine. It was not Cloud Eight and it was not Cloud Ten. It was Cloud Nine, the place where the women with helmeted bouffant hairdos dressed only in low white tennis shoes were devoted to pleasing a man by taking on themselves the odd combination of servitude and dominance that goes by the name of posing. Posing was at the essence of the control of women, he thought, and it was something that he had never known real women to be the least interested in, especially the Dark Actress.

As much as he secretly loved her, however, he would find his thoughts about her drifting toward Cloud Nine. He wondered if she even possessed a pair of low white tennis shoes. He doubted it, because she seemed to him a person of nobility and grace. She was not peppy, that was for sure, although she could be naked. Backstage, they would dress and undress together, the entire company, and he often saw her decorous little body, which seemed chaste and a far cry from the bountiful, helmet-headed women of Cloud Nine. One night, as the excellent and extravagant white-wigged actor who played King Lear carried her in his arms for her last scene—she dead, slain, her head draped backwards, he keening over her—the Dark Actress actually winked at Ballinger, or so he thought. He was amazed as he stood, legs firmly apart, holding between them a huge tree-trunk of a barbaric pole, its end stuck into the soft asphalt floor of the stage. Later, backstage, she never acknowledged the wink, not in any way. It might have been meant, he thought, for any of his companions, the faceless lot of supernumeraries who hoisted the banners and carried the spears.

Ballinger bemoaned his fate, he keened over it. He was lost somewhere between King Lear's miserable earth and the happiness of Cloud Nine. Earth was a place that had things like the House of Little Men among its tawdry addresses; a musty, creaky-floored place of lonely Japanese men living but temporarily in the bedrooms and alcoves, the living rooms and parlors of a place that must once have been filled with the homey chatterings and goings and comings of a large family; the men with handlebar mustaches, perhaps, the women in crinolines and parasols, their horses clacking up the cobbled streets, breathing out clouds of steam into the foggy air, the city but barely rebuilt from the great earthquake and fire, the early spider-like autos and panel trucks pulling up the steep hills. That family could not have imagined the Japanese loneliness into which their house would eventually drift. The House of Little Men, as the city had crowded in around it, had become crushed up next to a huge synagogue on the one side and row after row of similar houses, with not a foot between them, on the other. Most were now reduced to places for rent. They were slaves to the likes of Spook and they took it gracefully, as old gentlemen must. Spook roamed the house and the block, he buttonholed Jews and loomed over Japanese, he overlooked them all.

In later years, Ballinger would remember the tremendous dignity that Spook gave to every word and gesture, to every step and lunacy. He was a big man, probably young—he might have been thirty, he might have been forty—and he was said by everyone to work for The Mob—whatever that actually was—as a kind of pet, a runner perhaps. He certainly did not dress like a crazy person. He was sporty, in the kind of sharp-dressed, snap-brimmed, short-coated kind of look that was personified in those days by Sammy Davis, Jr. And he was mobile. He had a convertible, did Spook, a big old red Ford something-or-other, and he could quite deftly get it up and down the steep narrow driveway to the House of Little Men.

And, of most importance to Ballinger, he had a girlfriend. She was someone who, by appearance, you wouldn't have expected to be attached to someone as crazy as Spook. She was what was, in those primitive days, often called a big blonde bombshell—that is, she was something to look at. She was, as well, possessed of a big, forceful personality, to the point that Ballinger guessed that she must be the chief woman whom Spook would have to control in order to get on with his elaborate plan for dominating the moon and the earth.

Spook and the Blonde Bombshell would often wash the Big Red Convertible in the steep driveway and for this purpose they employed, of course, the standard garden hose. This hose, it turned out, was key to Spook's plan for controlling the world.

"WHEN YOU GET THE GUY ON THE MOON," Spook once shouted to Ballinger over the shrieking chainsaw (and once was enough), "THE GUY'S GONNA NEED AIR." Of course, a man had to live, a man had to breathe. Spook's solution was elegant and simple and based on modern technology—as modern as technology could be in the early Sixties of the Twentieth Century. If, he said, you had enough garden hoses, and linked them all together, you could get air to the moon through them; and you would thereby conquer the moon, control women, control men and, eventually, control what Spook liked to call the whole shooting match. The hose part of Spook's plan was unnerving to Ballinger. Spook was crazy, of course, and so his advice about women had to be taken with one or two cartons of salt.

But, on the other hand, Ballinger had to admit that none of the Little Men of California Street, however bravely each said he pursued the women of the town, knew much about them or any other women. Knowing about women was something reserved for older men, men who had been roughed up around the edges, men who had seen a few things, men like Mike Hammer or King Lear—or Spook, even. After all, Spook was much older than the rest of the residents of the House of Little Men and, besides, he worked for The Mob. It seemed natural, at the time, to at least listen to him for advice and ideas on the control of women.

Since Ballinger's thought was that the ultimate control of women was not marriage, was not even romance, but was to get them to pose—to be still and silent and full and waiting, as were the women of Cloud Nine—Spook's actual life gave the lie to much of what Spook said. Indeed, the Blonde Bombshell herself—gorgeous and voluptuous as she was—seemed to be a bossy kind of person who must have been in unnatural need of control and Spook must have been unable to provide it, that's what Ballinger thought. From his window he would watch the Blonde Bombshell sit in the Big Red Convertible in the steep driveway and loudly and publicly order Spook as to which spots to go over in the ritual washing of the car. She ordered Spook around, that was the simple fact of the matter, and she did it in public.

All of them inside the big house, each peering down from his Victorian window, whether from Honolulu or Kyoto or Fresno, were greatly taken with the Blonde Bombshell and each of them, he was sure, would have preferred her attentions directed upwards, where their little faces might be seen looking downward toward her mighty chest, which was exactly enhanced by the two-barreled, up-thrust fashions of the times.

The Blonde Bombshell, sitting imperiously in the Big Red Convertible, ordering Spook to get a spot here or a spot there, to polish this or that chrome, most emphatically did not pose. She was never still, she was never quiet and yet she was the closest woman by looks alone that Ballinger could imagine as equivalent to the women of Cloud Nine. She was a very platinum blonde. Her face—indeed, all of her, it seemed—was covered with a thick layer of peach-colored makeup. Her eyes were lined with dark paint, her eyelashes dripped mascara. She wore big hats to protect the makeup from the foggy sun. Her lips were painted a cherry red. She wore summer sundresses with big red polka-dots over bountiful petticoats. Her figure was the talk of the House of Little Men.

And then one day, just like that, Ballinger actually talked to the Blonde Bombshell and was alone with her, just the two of them, without the brooding and overpowering presence of Spook. It was an exciting moment for Ballinger. Needless to say—this being a story about real life—she did not pose, she did not stretch, she did not undress, she did not make love to him. She did not do what he wanted, whatever that was. In fact, she lectured him. He had mentioned his feelings, confused as they were, for the Dark Actress.

"Here's the deal, Ballinger," she said, or something to that effect. "You seem like a nice young boy, so it's about time someone told you a thing or two. Gals control the world." This Ballinger now had heard confirmed from two sources, and he was already inclined to believe it. The Blonde Bombshell was sitting in the Big Red Convertible talking to him from under her large straw hat. Her breasts sailed out in front of her. Spook was elsewhere, he knew not where.

"Gals," she said confidentially, "control the world by controlling the moon."

This was news to Ballinger. According to Spook, it was the other way around. It was the airless moon that controlled women.

"It's a gal thing," she said, letting implications of menstrual control hang in the air like the thick fog that was beginning to shade the little sun of that day. Ballinger looked down on her where her bountiful peach-colored flesh pressed against the slick, ribbed white seat covers of the Big Red Convertible.

"You're kidding," he said.

"I'm not kidding," she said. "It's monthly."

Ballinger was not a fool. He knew enough about the rudimentary science of the day to have discerned some connection between months and their namesake, the moon, as well as with the cycles of mystery experienced by women. "Cycles of Mystery" was a phrase favored by a shy hygiene teacher named Mrs. Florx whom he remembered from school in Fresno and whenever he heard it he would think of masked motorcycle riders whirring inside the wooden dromes of the county fairs of the Valley, the Cycles of Mystery. In fact, he found menstruation a dark subject, one usually kept carefully away from men. His own experience with women was so slight that he had never been made a part of the ritual secrets of it all. Now he had been admitted and in later years he would see that this was a great kindness to him on the part of the Blonde Bombshell, since no woman need admit any man into this, her most secret life.

That very night, at the performance of *King Lear*, he was given the second of the great kindnesses, and it came from the Dark Actress herself. She had fixed him with her beautiful eyes backstage during the non-stop action and wailings of actors and frantic quick-changings of heavy, sweaty leather costumes and in her case, long robes fashioned to reveal the tops of her perfect little breasts. He thought later that she must have sensed his love for her.

"Ballinger," she whispered, "I'm leaving the cast of this stupid play. I'm going down to Hollywood to be in the movies."

Years later he would figure out what she, in her kindness, was trying to tell him. She was going posing. She was going to have pictures taken of her. She was to be directed and her words and thoughts would be those of living writers and her exact dialogue could even be added on or manipulated later, after the posing was done. She was headed for Cloud Nine, in other words, and she wasn't going to take him along.

Like a sudden opening in his head, he realized certain things about life. Don't fall in love with actresses, for instance. Don't think that—however much you love the results—you can have anything to do with the nuts and bolts of posing. In other words, there are no men on Cloud Nine and peppiness has mostly to do with shoes and not real women.

"Well, Ballinger," his friend Akira Yoshida said to him one day soon after, after she had gone, "women are an unknown quantity. We don't know why they are as they are but they most certainly *are* as they are, that's for sure. I mean to say, they're not going to change."

"You know, Aki, that's probably wrong," said Ballinger. "Here's what I mean. The moon does not stay the same forever. In fact, once a month, regular as clockwork, it disappears entirely. It doesn't show itself at all on these certain nights. And on every other night of the month it is, indeed, a little bit different from every other night."

"Ah," said Aki after a pause, "like a woman."

And if you were up on her, safe up on the full moon with a shattered rocket by your side, breathing good California air out of a 5/8th-inch garden hose, it still wouldn't do you one damn bit of good, thought Ballinger, years later. You wouldn't even know how to start controlling her. In fact, a good case could be made that the moon herself had her own reasons for doing what she did. Perhaps those reasons had to do with going down to Hollywood and being in the movies. Maybe the moon needed the air or the publicity. Perhaps men like Spook were her instruments. Spook, creature of the moon. Perhaps Spook was working not for the great powers of earth, but for the moon herself, thought Ballinger. He was, perhaps, the ultimate traitor not only to his sex but to his very planet. The moon had figured out the kind of guy she'd need to exert her control over the earth and Spook was that guy.

In the House of Little Men, in San Francisco, many years ago more than Ballinger now cares to remember, as he looked back at a life that had been, he realized, almost entirely influenced, one way or another, by his yearnings and relations for and with one woman or another, significant things had happened to him, brought about by the kindnesses of women he could never hope to control.

After all, he thought, Cloud Nine must be a place set up very close to the moon, and probably for a very good reason.

The Age of Brass
A Tale of the Old Detective

☼

It was raining cats and dogs on a sultry day in my city, which is the City of the Queen of the Angels. The river in my city was rushing down its concrete channel to a nasty sea. My city has a name that sounds as if it ought to explain something, but it doesn't explain a thing.

"It's the Queen part that defies explanation," he had said when I talked to him on the phone. I could hardly hear him for the rain drumming my roof. "It always has defied explanation. It can't be the dogs and cats because they're everywhere, in every City."

What dogs and cats? I asked.

"It's raining dogs and cats," he said. "Didn't you just say that? Keep alert."

I hadn't phoned ahead that wet morning because he had called me to tell me he didn't have a phone anymore. I decided—from a certain tone in his voice I had come to recognize—that it was worth the trip and, later that day, found myself stepping up the wet red concrete steps of the tatty little pink and plaster bungalow apartment overhung by the flaming bougainvilleas lovingly cultivated by my ancient friend, the one I call the Old Detective, because he will not let me use his real name, which I have never frankly believed was his anyway. I was hoping he wanted to talk.

I knocked on his door. There was some sound I couldn't distinguish from inside. I pushed the old door open. I could hear him but I couldn't see him. His voice seemed to come from a shadowy collection of lumps slumped in an ancient armchair, backlit by rainy light from the fly-stained window.

"She was really something, this babe," said the voice.

"What babe?" I asked him. I found a place to sit and quietly reached for my notebook. Indeed, he seemed to want to talk.

"You see, it was a few years ago. I was still on the force, then. Those were bad times for me. I was awash in a sea of corruption, you might say."

I asked him how he was assigned.

"Archo, Hollywood Division. You know what it's like. Running errands for the brass hats, waiting for my chance to pull the brass ring, polishing the brass monkey—you get the point."

I told him that I didn't think I got the point.

"Sure, you're a pretty smart guy. How much does it take? How many repetitions of the word 'brass' do you need before it begins to sink in?"

I kept silent. It hadn't sunk in.

"I never had a normal life, not ever. Oh, maybe once or twice some woman would get to me. Well, to tell you the truth, this was one of those times. I met her on a dark night when I was sent out on a three-oh-nine." He looked up at me expectantly. When I didn't answer, he said: "That's archo code for a homicide that takes place in the Brass Age."

He didn't look like he was kidding, but I told him I thought he was. He looked at me as if I was the one of us crazy as a bat-rabbit. He sighed and lit up a cigarette.

"Where have you been? When I was your age, I'd seen it all before. The Brass Age. Big deal. Usually some scummy incident down by the tracks…a few shards of broken pottery, some nondescript copper or brass bracelets worth nothing in a town already overloaded with tar-pit treasures. Sabre-tooth tiger skulls were so common that every street-corner back then had a museum with a big old red ice tub for soda pop outside on the porch."

I said I hadn't known that.

"You're too young," he said. "They were the kind of tubs where you'd reach down into the ice and water and fish around in the Delaware Punches and Shasta Colas and Royal Crowns and so forth and finally pull out an ice-cold green little bottle filled with..." His old voice trailed off.

"Coke?" I asked, as politely as possible.

"No, thanks," he said distractedly. "The stuff just shoots up through my nose and lodges in my brain."

The cicadas called outside, like little pieces of electricity gone wrong. A hot wind had blown the drizzle here. The screen door banged open and shut twice. Somewhere a siren wailed.

"The point being?" I said.

"That this was a rotten town in those days."

"Brass age days?" I thought I'd humor him.

"You got that right, little man. Days of unalloyed terror, beaten days, paint-your-body kind of days."

He didn't seem to think it was at all funny when I asked him if he didn't mean "Paint Your Wagon" days?

"Do I? Don't be a sap. They didn't have stupid Broadway musicals in the Brass Age. The Brass Age was a time of somber reflection and furtive imagining. It was a time of little dark plays in cabarets and entertainment that consisted, for the most part, in burying guys alive in swamps clothed in rotting pieces of fiber. Give me a break. Get a life. Those expressions were invented in the Brass Age."

I thought about this for a moment and then I decided to keep taking notes. Maybe, I thought, there was something in this. I asked him to tell me more about the girl because she seemed like the best lead for a story.

"She was something, all right. She was great looking, but in a kind of haughty way. She was one of those high-born dames with a lot of jewelry socked away and an eye for men with shipping fortunes."

I was writing as fast as I could.

"What kind of jewelry?" I asked.

"It should have been brass jewelry." He had a slight smile on his face, but I didn't write that down. "You see, they hadn't invented diamonds and pearls yet in the Brass Age. People had a different set of values."

"I'll bet."

"Not in the Brass Age, you wouldn't. Gambling was strictly illegal, see? I told you, a different set of values." He leaned forward in his chair now, angling himself so a shaft of drowned light played down over his battered features. He was wearing his detective hat and he seemed extraordinarily pleased with himself.

"I was surprised when I got to the scene of the outbreak," he said expansively. "It wasn't just the usual senseless shards of tattered ancient flax. There was a body this time. He looked to be a little guy, from what we could tell. A femur and a tibia for the worse, some charcoal remains in his withered stomach. With bark for shoes, the guy couldn't have been more than five feet tall. Someone croaked him, I had just said, when Lefty—one of the guys from downtown—said he'd found this babe out in the parking lot looking at herself in the side mirrors of the cars. She was wild and angry, and shouting things in what sounded to me to be French. I took her inside a squad car to ask her a few questions. It was dark inside, just the moonlight slanting in the windows and some of it slid down over her body like it knew what it was doing. She had on diamonds and pearls and they glinted in the pale light." The Old Detective paused for a distant moment. His eyes seemed wet. "She was something to look at, did I say that? She was exotic, all right, and she looked like she came from somewhere far off, but not somewhere where ages are named after metals, if you see what I mean."

I thought I saw what he meant. I asked him where she had come from, if not the Brass Age.

"I found out later—too late, really—that she came from the Age of Reason, which seemed reasonable enough until you got to know her. But at first I didn't know her and so I accepted her story. It was the usual crap, you know, how she couldn't have done it because she was from the Age of Reason, which, as everyone knows, is a long way forward from the Age of Brass plus being more, you know, reasonable."

I took a deep breath and told him that a lot of people, while they might agree on his assessment of chronology, would still find it hard to believe in her actual existence.

"Listen, people existed back then, don't you worry about it." He was practically shouting.

I made my voice sound cheerful. I hadn't meant to hurt his feelings. I asked him what the dame looked like.

"Oh, not much," he said, moodily. "Like every little moonbeam, dancing on a star. Like spring nights and the smell of gardenias and jaguars. You get the point. She was a knockout. And I was always, in those days, a sucker for those big white wigs and a lot of cleavage and makeup plastered on with a trowel. And moles. She had a big one although it turned out it wasn't real. She was carrying a shepherd's crook, too. She seemed like she had an airtight alibi until it turned out there was some sheep dip in the clay and loam composition soil that the boys had already dug out around the body and sifted through by the time I got to the scene. But still, something just didn't fit for me. I had that feeling I get. It didn't make sense that a dame from the Age of Reason—especially this dame—would kill the Ice Man."

"The body?" I said. "You called him the Ice Man?"

"Everyone called him that."

"That's great," I said and then I asked why it was that everyone had called him that since from what I had heard so far he wasn't found frozen or anything. It might rain little green apples in L.A., but it doesn't freeze them.

"Why he was called the Ice Man? That was his name—at least it was his professional name. His actual name was Chuck. Turned out he had an ice cream truck and a regular route and was known as 'The Ice Man' for years around North Hollywood and parts of Glendale. You'd have to go far in the homicide game to find a name with as much appeal to the press mob as 'The Ice Man,'" he said proudly.

I asked him if there had been a lot of coverage.

"No. Hell, she just laid 'em out there for anyone to see. She didn't even have a sweater. It's the way they did things in the Age of Reason, she said, and she told me to just get used to it and be reasonable. She had this imperious way about her and so I started calling her Queenie, way before it really took hold with the press hounds."

I said that it sounded to me as if he might have been falling for her.

"You might say that and you might not."

I mentioned that I had said that and he paused for a long minute. After awhile, he said softly:

"After the interrogation, I took her out for a drink to a little place I know that makes little drinks and we slugged back about two hundred highballs each and she cried on my shoulder for a while. In those days, my heart wasn't made of brass, the way it is now."

I asked him what it was made of.

"It was made of some other kind of poop that just melted away as she wept. She said she was the Queen of Los Angeles and I could see her point. She was something to look at, this one. I figured, okay, she meant, you know, like she was Queen of the Racetrack or Queen for a Day or Cantaloupe Queen of L.A. or something like that but she said no, she was the actual Queen of the Angels and she hadn't croaked the Ice Man at all because angels were, by definition, incapable of murder. I said well, okay, if you're the Queen, where are the rest of the angels? 'What?' she says. The other angels, I says, the ones you're the Queen of. That stopped her. 'Oh,' she said, 'they're...around, I guess,' and she gestured vaguely out toward Hollywood Boulevard. I got suspicious then, because the implications were pretty clear to me, no matter what my heart was saying."

"Those implications being...?"

"That she was lying. There hadn't been an angel on Hollywood Boulevard in a hundred and fifty years, when Frenchmen used to make movies out there with rubber film and people running in front of the lens fast to create flickering. And here was the kicker, she *looked* exactly like the Queen of France, see? No Queen of Angels would wear a dress cut that low, no Queen of Angels would giggle and use a fan and pretend to herd sheep and wear a fake mole. I was dealing with the Queen of France here and no matter how much she locked those liquid blues on mine, no matter how hard my heart raced every time I looked at her, I still had to face the facts. Queens of France, you see, are traditionally above the law. They can murder pretty much anyone they want to, for instance."

"Whereas a Queen of Angels would presumably obey some higher law?"

"You got that right. The laws of our city, such as they were in those days. But then, those were corrupt days. There were really only two laws: walk or don't. I figured the key to the case was the Ice Man himself."

"Chuck?"

"Don't laugh. He paid his taxes, he was licensed by the city of North Hollywood. But there he was, most definitely from the Age of Brass. He probably left grieving relatives behind with bark shoes stuffed with reeds and carrying leather satchels with grains of wheat and corn or maybe even a coal of fire. He was living in the Brass Age, no matter what he did in North Hollywood during business hours. He couldn't have been really that comfortable here in the Age of Electricity, or whatever it's called now. He couldn't have been."

I said I had read recently that the Age of Electricity was over and we were now in something called the Age of Agitation.

"Ah," he pondered. "I thought we were maybe up to the Age of Alignment by now. That's the Age where you won't have to rotate your tires every two weeks."

I asked him what had happened.

"What happened? Oh yeah, I forget. You're too young. It was in all the papers. They nailed her, but good. It was all over the front pages to the point that a mob of peasants—peasants mostly lived in Glendale in those days—stormed the County Jail because she made that famous statement to the press that she enjoyed eating jail food and she felt sorry for the rest of 'le monde'—that's the way she talked—who couldn't eat tortillas. 'Let them eat sponge cake,' she said. 'I like a nice tostada here in jail,' she said, 'it's healthy...' And then she'd pause and say: 'Con huevos.' She pretty much had her way with the print boys. They parroted everything she said. She could put those tostadas away, too. She must have ballooned up to about a hundred and seventy, before the end came."

I asked him if that meant that she had been fried, you know, had her last meal, downed her last cigarette, taken that lonesome walk to oblivion, done the voltage dance, inhaled the green cloud, had her neck stretched like a rubber band.

"Yeah, she walked all right," he said, puffing a cloud of smoke. He was smoking just the filters now. "She just plain walked right out of jail. The judge gave her some money out of his own pocket, with tears in his eyes, in fact, and then awarded her the Ice Man's old route. She built it up, franchised it, put in thirty-some flavors—including a Taco Almond Crunch that's still popular. You get the picture."

I got the picture.

"Queenie's still around," he said. "Lives up in Paso Robles, married a vintner, has a big vineyard, has cheese-tasting parties, the whole bit. Probably has a Range Rover," he muttered grumpily. "She never called me, never again."

Well, I said after a pause, maybe Queens of France from the Age of Reason don't know about the tough and guarded love of a modern guy since they're used to a kind of adoration usually reserved for singers and actors.

"Maybe," he said, moodily. "Maybe you're right. She picked up modern life fast, believe me. Too fast. You see, that's why I finally figured out that the judge was right. Okay, so she was from the Age of Reason, so she had a philosophical attitude about things we take seriously, like murder. But she had no comprehension of the Brass Age. Old for her meant bringing in some French guys with leather aprons to build fake Roman ruins in the back garden. She didn't have a clue about modern life or ancient life. She had no motive whatsoever. No, I always thought it was more likely that the Ice Man croaked himself. That's the kind of pressure modern life would put on a guy from the Brass Age, if you see what I mean."

I supposed I saw what he meant. I knew one thing, though. He was surely talking about a time in our town in the days before plastic, when wood was wood and metal was metal and you talked to people with copper wire strung between you and everything had thick black cords that plugged into the wall. It was before diesel, before foreign cars, before the Age of Agitation, before the pressure started in on us for serious. It was a day of rosy sunrises over the mountains above Glendale and the old pepper trees swaying in the Santa Ana winds against the brass sunsets of yesteryear.

That's the way I like to think it was, anyway, in those twilight days of our town, the City of The Queen of the Angels, who turned out to be a babe who once, long ago, fell in love with the Old Detective, if only for a Brass Age moment.

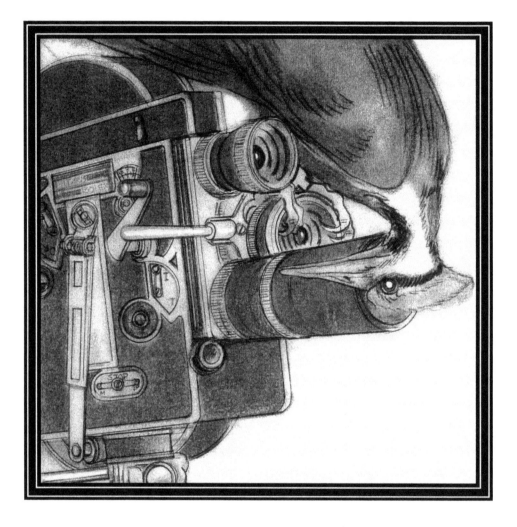

Ed Woodpecker, Private Eye

✧

Chapter 1

It was hot for once, for one damned day up here in the Far North. Tacoma (The City of Arson) lay smoldering in this mighty heat, down below me, down there in what we like to call The City of Destiny, no matter how stupid other people might think we are. In the old days, Tacoma—up here in the State of Washington—was said to smell bad, especially by the jealous citizens of Seattle. They said the smell was overwhelming, something like a couple of football fields' worth of two-day dead geoducks smoldering on a bed of burning cow pies. They had quite a flair for language in the old days, up in Seattle, but now it was different. Tacoma was nice now, it was a nice place, the pulp mills gone and with them the mighty smell. The town was gone too, but if it had been there, it would have been nice enough.

It was a nice enough day, too, although it was hot as hell. I'll let you know right from the beginning that I'm a Tacoma guy myself, a T-town lifelong resident. I've even got an office up in the old Rust Building down on Pacific Avenue and I've got two windows in that office and one of them looks one way and one looks the other. Neither shows me the desolation of Downtown Tacoma (The Downtown of Lost Hope), for reasons I'll try to explain.

On slow days—and I've had a couple—a lot of people ask me (more people than you'd think) how a woodpecker like me got into the private eye business. I tell them that the Woodpeckers, at least my branch of them, are an old detective family in Taco Town. We go way back, in other words. My dad Woodrow was a detective before he went down to Hollywood and got so famous, and his mother and most of my cousins and my twin sisters were all detectives. Most of us were in the detective business, is what I mean to say, that is, the bunch of us who grew up around Snake Lake. We pecked around, we stuffed things in holes and hoped to find them again. We tapped out messages. We packed a piece. We climbed transoms. We never—never—worked for the heat. They wouldn't have a woodpecker on the force, they said, even if hell froze over and the woodpeckers had the only acetylene torch in town. (This is unlikely. For instance, it takes about three hundred woodpeckers just to do a decent weld with an acetylene torch and to my knowledge hasn't been attempted since 1938 when the shipbuilding business was booming locally. Incidentally, it's a fool of an arsonist who has to use an acetylene torch, as my uncle Woodman used to say.)

On this day, this hot day—did I mention that?—I kicked closed the bottom drawer of my desk, the one with the nearly empty bottle of Old Hercules in it, and looked idly through every chamber of my rod. I couldn't afford the Federal tax on ammo, so I'd packed the chambers full of acorns and pine nuts. I might be virtually unarmed, but I wasn't going to go hungry. It was too early for lunch. If I'd had a secretary, I would have insisted she call herself Frankie.

"Hey Frankie, " I would have yelled to her over the intercom, "what's on the agenda for today, baby?"

"Well, boss," she would have said breathily, crossing her leggy gams, "there's that little matter of the Missing Downtown. You were going to call it the Case of the Missing Downtown, in fact."

"Oh, yeah," I would have said. I would have remembered, then, oh yeah, I would say to myself, there's that little matter of the entire downtown business section just disappearing out of view. Yeah, I would have thought. I've got to get on top of that one.

I pushed aside the tattered curtain with my foot and looked out one window. Sure enough, the guy had been right. Where Downtown Tacoma had once been, draped over the seven hills, there was nothing, nothing at all.

Chapter 2

The Rust Building was still there, otherwise what building was I in? But the rest of downtown was missing. A lot more was missing; Frankie, for instance. Oh, some people were around. Some birds, as well. They were all right. The people, though, wandered aimlessly. You couldn't hear a phone ring. You couldn't start your car if it was in Downtown Tacoma. I could look down from my office on the top floor and see people staring at their cars, hands in their pockets, if they had pockets, if they had cars. I stared down at them and after awhile tried to make a couple of calls. Nothing. The phones were on, but there were no rings and no dial tones and you could only hear anonymous voices talking about how they couldn't get anyone on the phone, except, of course, for the people they were talking to, none of whom seemed to be downtown, and none of whom seemed to be able to get downtown because it had evidently disappeared, just the way the guy had said.

Earlier that morning, I'd heard a voice. It wasn't Frankie's voice, that was for sure.

"Hello. Anyone around?"

There was a guy out in my empty reception area. I tried not to look at Frankie's little plaid coat still waiting for her to come back as I let him in to the inner sanctum. The guy was regular-looking, a middle-aged white human in a checked suit that must have had Sears all agog in 1977, but when he handed me his embossed card, I suddenly got that solid feeling a detective gets when he knows he's got a client who's going to be able to pay the fee. His card told me he was a guy from down on Pacific Avenue. Most important, he was the owner of a place called the Eye Shoppe, and that place was a goldmine, as I'd heard tell my whole life. Old men in Tacoma said there were things in the Eye Shoppe that could sense the stars, that could see clear into the wings of a wasp, that could plumb the depths of the Sound and the far reaches of the night sky, that could stop Time in his tracks. This guy was muscular, with the weight of the known world pushing down his businessman's shoulders. His card, embossed as it was, told me his name was E.Z. Haag.

"Well, Ed," E.Z. Haag said, settling himself into my good chair, "it's bad, Ed. Downtown seems to be gone, pretty much. For instance, there's no one down on Pacific Avenue anymore except grifters and no-goods and bankers and very few of them want cameras. Between you and me, I can see their point. Why would you need a camera if you live in a cardboard box and can't even afford to go to the Harbor Lights Restaurant for lunch every day? But it's still no damn reason to disappear everything."

"I get it. You're in the camera business." I lit up a Lucky.

"Yeah," he snarled, leaning forward and fixing me with his steely fixative of a gaze. "It's called the Eye Shoppe and eye is a camera, get it? Except nowadays, people seem to think that cameras should be digital or made of cardboard and be able to be just thrown away after one use."

"Very small grifters and no-goods could live in them then," I said helpfully.

"What?"

"Bankers. Small bankers, maybe. Never mind. Go on."

"There was a day in this town, Woodpecker, when cameras told the story. Men used to run from cameras. If you had a camera you might have all sorts of evidence. For instance," and here he looked furtively around, "maybe the Galloping Gertie Bridge fell down one fine day."

"You're kidding," I said, leaning forward and glancing from side to side and lighting up a Lucky with the Lucky I already had burning. This was news to me.

"I'm not kidding," he said, seriously enough. "I've got the proof—or at least I did have the proof until someone walked off with Downtown Tacoma and took my negatives with it. There was more, too, lots more. There were naked local babes and pictures of arsonists, lots of secrets of the town." His voice got faraway and he had a gone look in his eye. Abruptly, he threw some money on the desk. "Help me," he said and then he got up and went away.

I had nothing else on my plate, after all, and I could see hundreds in the bills he'd thrown down. I was a Woodpecker, after all, and certain traditions run deep. I tried not to think of the deep tradition of stupidity that ran down my family tree like a lightening scar. It was probably as deep in our family as sapsucking or woodpecking or an interest in homicidal acts.

"I'm all yours, E. Z." I said, but he had gone.

What was that he'd said? The Galloping Gertie Bridge might have even fallen down?

I climbed out on my windowsill and took off and flew over to the 11th Street Bridge and sat up on one of the towers and did woodpecker things for awhile, avoiding the question. Woodpecker things have mostly to do with preening and wondering if it's lunchtime yet. After awhile I forced myself to look at it out of the corner of the eye on that side, which looks pretty much sideways anyway. What a relief, there it was, the big old green bridge, the double-poled monstrosity that somehow binds the Olympic Peninsula and Tacoma in a marriage of profound uncertainty. Galloping Gertie, she was called by everyone. You could drive over the Galloping Gertie Bridge, but she swayed treacherously from side to side, she buckled and rolled and rumbled. You'd be driving your bread truck, say (if you drove a bread truck), from Gig Harbor over to Tacoma and the bridge would be galloping so hard that you'd be driving up a shaky asphalt hill and you'd see the car in front of you literally disappear down another. Kids used to dare each other just to walk across it. It was huge, it must span a mile, I guessed. When I thought about it, there was probably some small chance it might fall down, but it had never really occurred to me or anyone else in Tacoma. Tacoma is, after all, the City of Optimism (The City of False Hopes) and we don't go around looking for trouble. It just seems to find its way here, although how it could do that with the bridge fallen down I couldn't see. This guy E.Z. Haag was obviously crazy, I thought. All I had to do was stretch this case out over a couple of weeks and collect a few more hundreds and all would be well. I flew back to the Rust Building and dove in my window and sat at my desk for a while and then I went down and tried to start my car but none of the keys I had fit anywhere in it. I tried to talk to some people who were just aimlessly standing around with nowhere to go, but a lot of Tacomans have a hard time talking to a woodpecker. I'm used to it. I flew off and sailed up in the air and launched myself out over the bay.

I love the Great Northwest. I'll say it now and I'll say it again. It's just entrancing that the sea makes a big dish in the land and the land is covered with great trees and grass and everything green. There were a lot of seagulls around as usual and even some kingfishers over on Fox Island. No eagles in sight. I landed in Gig Harbor near where those geese nest in the big wine-cask barrels out on the Tides Tavern deck and I ordered up the Halibut and Chips and Pound O' Fries and a pitcher of Alaskan Amber and sat outside overlooking the dock and counted the starfish and ate and drank beer and threw the seagulls some fries. I had to think and seagulls quiet down considerably when they're eating French fries. Here's what I was thinking:

That there's a thin line between humans and birds, and one of the places on earth where that line hits the ground is in Tacoma. You could fall in love with a human, if you were a bird, and this is the place in all the world where the romance would have a better than normal chance of at least lasting a week or two. You could murder a bird, or a bird could murder you, and there was a good chance of the cops paying attention for a couple of weeks. Why this was so, I didn't have a clue. But I'd noticed it was true and I'd be the one to ask, if you were in a questioning mood, even though I wouldn't be able to give you much of an answer.

On top of that, the client agreed with me on at least one thing, the downtown was missing, even though we lived in it, we were a part of it, part of the fabric of it, in fact. But then we parted company. He saw the bridge down and I saw it up. He seemed to not know the difference between humans and birds exactly. I looked over at the Galloping Gertie Bridge and much to my surprise, there it lay in a crumpled, submerged heap, most of it sunk to the bottom of the Tacoma Narrows. The bridge was down. The guy had been right. The human had booked me on a genuine case. Most of my jobs the last few years had been bird jobs, the usual stuff, hummingbird murders, mobbing mayhems, small-bore, three-day cases.

You're probably thinking by now that an entire pitcher of beer in the middle of the day should be too much for one woodpecker, and you'd be right as far as that went, which wouldn't be far enough. For a capitalized Woodpecker, it isn't half enough beer. There's a difference, you see.

It was hot, did I mention that? I had thought enough, or so I thought. I had to get started and since the job was, as I understood it, to find out what happened to all the stuff that was in the Eye Shoppe, including confusing negatives and something about naked local Babes, then there was only one place to start and that was in the Downtown of Tacoma which had disappeared—for some—as well. The peripheral issues…why some saw a bridge and some didn't, why it was so hot, where Frankie had got to, why some lived and why some died…would have to wait.

I flew back toward T-town, but first I set down on Mystery Island and stopped in at this big old fir tree that looked vaguely familiar, something I thought maybe I'd been fond of when I was a kid and so I took the time and looked for some stuff I might have left uneaten or left forgotten. There was something I'd pecked into holes there, from when I was a kidling. Nothing much was left; some caps from a cap pistol of long ago, barely intact, a moldy old bug, inedible. I flew back toward Tacoma, bloated and still thinking when someone took a shot at me.

Chapter 3

The shot missed me, that's the long and short of it. It was a little long or maybe a little short, but it just whacked a couple of my tail feathers and screamed off into the Northwest air, to land with some plunk in the Sound, I supposed. I was so shocked. I was frightened. I had that horrible feeling anyone gets when they are threatened. I panted. I dropped and whirled and fell and pulled up and looked around and tried to figure where it came from and breathed real hard and panted some more and maybe whimpered some because somebody taking a shot at you never gets any easier, no matter how many times it's been tried, no matter how tough you've convinced yourself you are. I thought, for a moment, that I had probably spent way too much of my life convincing myself of things that were not true, that were not right.

I flew up high and top-arced and got some speed going and dove down in a long slant over the dead flat calm bay toward Tacoma. I looked ahead and sure enough, the downtown was just as gone as the

Bridge, but it wasn't crumpled and destroyed. It was just gone. I was sort of scared. Everything else was there; the Brown's Point Light, Point Defiance, Point No Point, all the local points were still there. It was just the downtown area that seemed to be gone, or had a mist just appeared? It would have to be a pretty thick and pretty localized mist, I thought. It was hard to think where mist would come from on the hottest day of the year anyway. I began to pull up as I crossed the Thea Foss Waterway, watching carefully, as only a bird in the air can, and as I slowed, as I banked down, suddenly, dimly, the downtown emerged, its clock tower, its railroad past; it emerged, indeed, like something rising from out of a mist that wasn't even there. I could see the downtown, the old train station, the Glass Sculpture Bridge, the bums by the Greyhound Bus station. Towering above it all, making a peak to it, was the ironwork tower and the copper roof of the old familiar Rust Building and I flew up to the top floor and sure enough, there was my old familiar office. I looked at my phone and my filing cabinets made of old madrone wood and the little reception room where Frankie didn't sit anymore. I took a deep breath and turned around on the window sill and looked out over the bay and there was the bridge, as intact and complete and as right as anything real. Well, I thought to myself, we seem to have a mystery here.

A woodpecker, after all, is so often looking for things he's already hidden away that I had the creeping feeling that I was to blame somehow. Had I pecked a big hole and put downtown Tacoma in it and then just forgotten all about it? Had I made enemies whom I'd stuffed away and forgotten? I ate a few pine nuts out of the chambers of my old .38, then I ate all the acorns and found some ammo and loaded it up and put it in my back pocket and went to the Men's Room. There was only me among the old tiles. The sun slanted in the window. It must have been a hundred degrees in there. For a woodpecker, those old-fashioned stand-up urinals are a godsend. I took the elevator to the lobby and walked down to The Eye Shoppe on Pacific Avenue. I try not to fly around town, it makes people nervous.

"Ed," said E.Z. Haag, sitting behind the counter, sweltering, "I'm depressed. You don't seem to be getting the job done."

"A job like this takes a lot of thinking," I said grimly. "Besides, you only hired me this morning." I looked around and indeed, The Eye

Shoppe had been cleaned out; not a camera, not a lens, not a telescope, not a roll of film in the place.

"When did the bridge fall down?" I asked.

"It was years ago, I think," he said. "I remember my father talking about it. It twisted loose in the wind. I have the negatives he shot, or I did have them. There was some sixteen millimeter film, black-and-white, and a roll of color as well. There wasn't a date on anything, though. But it was years ago. There's a conspiracy to keep it hidden from us."

"To keep hidden from us that there is no actual bridge there?"

"That's right," he said somewhat defiantly.

"What have we been driving on since then," I asked reasonably. "What have we been seeing there? I don't use it much, but it seems to *be* there. I'm not hearing any complaints from the public."

"Read the Gig Harbor paper, such as it is. They don't see a bridge there," he said glumly. "Check it out. There's lots of things in this town that aren't there anymore. Whatever happened to those little green bags your burger came in at the Frisko Freeze, for instance? Where's that nightclub down on the shorefront that was made from an old ship?"

He had a point. These things had mystified me as well.

"For instance, people who leave downtown Tacoma these days never seem to come back," he said. "The downtown population is getting smaller and smaller. The drugstore counter downstairs in the Rust Building has run out of tuna fish and Cokes. Some businessmen, unable to deal with their cars, just walk away and never return. If you look in the phone book, they just aren't listed anymore."

"Cars were never listed in the phone book," I said.

"The people, they aren't listed anymore."

"Oh," I said. I knew what he meant. My whole floor on the Rust Building was empty except for me. I hadn't had a tuna fish sandwich and a Coke in over a month. One minute I saw a bridge and the next I saw it fallen. People were leaving and that's probably what had happened to my secretary, Frankie. She'd walked out, high heels and all, and she'd never returned.

I knew something had been bothering me, on top of everything else, on top of being shot at. Frankie was gone, and I'd been trying to convince myself that she'd never even existed.

Chapter 4

Frankie existed somewhere in that gray area between humans and birds, of that I was sure. I just wasn't sure how to get there, although you'd think I'd be the one with the map. I'd better point out, as well, that Frankie was a dame like no other dame I'd ever known. She was really something. She looked like everything you ever imagined wouldn't be yours, ever. She had eyes like the deep night sky. She had lips that were the two lips of doom. She had legs that went up to the top floor, maybe beyond. The rest of her, as we detectives like to say, wasn't bad either. What Frankie was doing in Tacoma, the City of the Future (the City of Going Nowhere), I could never figure out, to tell you the truth. She might have left years ago. She might have been wearing expensive dresses with shifty hemlines and shoulder pads a mile wide. She might have had on black lipstick and no underwear in Spain. She might have had the world on a plate, might Frankie, and yet she'd wound up working for Ed Woodpecker, Private Eye, in the Rust Building, high above a town that was too little and too late for the likes of someone like her. I didn't get it. And besides, it seemed she didn't even work for me anymore. It had been several days now and she hadn't been back, hadn't called. The handwriting was on the wall, although I didn't want to read it.

We hadn't been getting along, Frankie and me, I guess you might say. There was that little matter of me asking her to marry me and her refusing, or at least maintaining a kind of silence that stones might envy. After that incident, she wouldn't even go downstairs and have lunch with me anymore, claiming that there was no tuna fish down there and that she liked a Coke with her lunch and, besides, the seats at the lunch counter didn't turn around smoothly anymore. I couldn't argue with her, although I tried. There was that little matter of her being bothered because I was a woodpecker and she—theoretically, anyway—wasn't. Theoretically, there was a theory, but I hadn't been let in on it. The line between woodpeckers and humans is a thin one, as far as I'm concerned. All I could think of was the way, in happier times, she'd twirl lazily on the easy-turning aluminum stools down at the lunch counter of the Rust Building, her high heels strapped around her ankles, her little plaid skirts floating in the breeze, laughing as we ate tuna fish and drank Cokes, vanilla in my case and plain in hers.

Finally, I went through her desk. There was nothing in there except a couple of old copies of *W* magazine and some female makeup implements I wasn't exactly sure of the uses for. Stuck in one corner was a newspaper ad for something going on at the Tacoma Dome tonight. I could only read the date and not what the event was. Maybe she'd be there. Hmmm, I thought. (That's the way I think.) I should pursue the money, find the Missing Downtown and solve the mystery of the looting of the Eye Shoppe, or I could look for my girl, the one girl I've ever loved, the girl of all my dreams—even the bad ones. Look for the woman, that's what French detectives say, as if they didn't have better things to do, which they don't. I didn't either, I thought. E.Z. Haag would have to wait, I thought.

The Dome is one of several interesting things about Tacoma (The City of Interesting Things). It's made of wood, number one, and that's a fact that's bound to get any woodpecker's attention. It's huge, it's big, I thought. Right then, someone smacked me hard right in the back of my woodpecker head. My thoughts stopped right then and there.

Woodpeckers have heads that are designed to hammer holes in wood and so are a kind of combination of a maul and an adze. Luckily, whoever it was hit me on the maul part and so my head snapped forward sharply and the adze part unfortunately drilled my bill so far into my desk that when I came to, I couldn't lift my head up at all. My bill must have been stuck a full two inches into old alder. Even semi-conscious, woodpeckers are famous for peripheral vision. Woozy as I was, I could easily see that there was no one holding a gun on me. There was no one there at all, in fact. I twisted my bill around and back and forth and eventually got the point out and then I rubbed the back of my head which had a big knot on it. I opened my bill more than a few times to make sure it worked and when it did, I took a fistful of aspirin from Frankie's bottom drawer and staggered out to the elevator and then down to the street. I needed to drink. I didn't need to think.

I staggered to the Point, a new bar on one of those old blocks that come to a sharp triangle point in Tacoma. I drank myself silly there. No one talked to me, not even Parky, the barkeep. He stared at me, though. He stared at me good.

"Hey. Woodpecker," he said after awhile.

"Yeah, what?" I growled.

"I've got a question for you. What would you think? Think about it. I hear things in here. Now, the other day, a little bird told me something…"

"There are no small birds, only small parts for birds," I said. "No bird has had a good part in a movie since *The Crow* or *The Birds*."

"I'm not talking about the movies, I'm talking about a little bird that was in here the other day. The little guy was drunk and cryin' his eyes out."

"A wren? A pee-wit? An Empidonax flycatcher?"

"How the hell would I know? He had some yellow on him, under his throat, maybe."

"Ah. A warbler."

"Could have been, could not have been. Like I say, I don't give a flying fuck at the moon and a half. Birds come, birds go. Between you and me and a hole in the Dome, most of 'em require, you know, a swipe of the bar rag across the stool, if you know what I mean, I mean, begging your sympathy and all, not that you have any problem, you know what I mean."

I knew what he meant, but I ignored it. "What was the little guy cryin' about?" I asked as if I didn't really care.

"You hear a lot behind this bar," he said meditatively. I reached in my pocket—I have a pocket—and found a couple of bills with numbers on them he liked.

"He was worried about the Dome," said Parky brightly, pocketing the cash. "A lot of birds are worried about the Dome, or so it seems."

"Yeah?

"Yeah. You hear it all around. Haven't you heard it all around? I mean from birds. Humans don't give a flying fuck, frankly."

"Have you seen Frankie around?

"You're like a broken record, Woodpecker. Isn't that frankly-Frankie joke ever going to stop fascinating you?"

"Don't give me a lot of shit, Parky. Stick to the subject."

"The subject being…?"

"The subject being that I gave you money to give me information. What do the birds fear or hope about the Tacoma Dome?"

"The little guy didn't say. That's all I know. That's my information. Want your money back?" He looked tough and determined. I didn't want my money back. I didn't want to fight. I just wanted Frankie back.

I staggered outside and straightened myself up and I walked the few blocks up through the old brick warehouses to the TacomaDome. The back of my head still hurt like hell.

Chapter 5

Let's face the facts. Someone had taken a shot at me. Someone had hit me on the head. Whoever it was had gone undetected by me, a professional detective. This was not good. None of it was good.

I slipped across the parking lot and pushed inside the huge wooden shell through a hole, one of the first holes, a hole my dad was reputed to have first pecked when he was but a fledgeoid. (Woodpeckers have amazingly short life spans if you talk to humans, who use an entirely different numbering and time system than woodpeckers do.) I squeezed inside the mighty wooden edifice and looked around, I could see that the Dome was full that night. It looked like a sports crowd, maybe boxing, because I didn't see any babes around. The whole vast Dome was full of the kind of guys you can see anytime around Tacoma, but only rarely in one place—without babes. I could see that some of the biggest wigs of a town known for its bigwigs were there: the Harbormaster, for instance, the head of the Water Company, the Amusement King. I knew a lot of these guys from as far back as High School.

And most amazing of all, they all rose up and shouted and raised their arms in unison. Most of them raised two arms, in point of fact. Some of them raised each other's arms. They shouted out that they would take care of their families' values.

"I *will* take out the garbage," they shouted. "I *will* spend more time with the kids." They wanted to let the world know that they were not going to be Deadbeat Dads. They did the Wave. They danced the dance, they moved the moves. There was a feeling of raw emotion and unbridled brotherly commitment surging through them, as if two opposing football teams had fallen in love, each with the other and had each just got up nerve enough to ask for a first date.

Up on the stage of the Dome, a voice thundered out to them. A big fat man was shouting out over the booming sound system:

"We want to be sensitive! We want to celebrate, c'mon, yeah, yeah!" I couldn't make out every word. The sounds seemed to overlap in waves of misunderstanding.

"We're guys! We think women are fascinating! But Lord God, doesn't it make you weep to understand that we are not women? No, we can never be women, even though we think they are the greatest things in the world. They produce children at literally the drop of a hat but we do not want them to come to these rallies! They'd just be in the way! Women are the sort of people who wouldn't understand the true difference between a real Frisko Freeze Burger and the sodden imitation being sold in this very dome! The emotions engendered by all this male bonding would be too much for them. OH, GOD! OH, JESUS! I will, *I will*, keep my promises to their sacred and fecund selves!" They panted and shouted and wept and raised their arms. It was manly and yet it was embarrassing. Ah, I thought. (That's the way I sometimes think.) So these were the Seekers I'd heard so much about. Why would Frankie have wanted to come here on this night, or if she wasn't going to be there—and I could see she wasn't—why was she even interested in these idiots? I noticed that up behind the big fat man there was a huge projection screen. Images came and went upon its face, sometimes the crowd would see itself, sometimes the speakers on the stage, sometimes they would see scenes from the area projected, birds of the area, for example, flying over the various scenic points. Birds. A few Seekers had begun to notice the images of birds massed, pushing against the Galloping Gertie Bridge; of birds, massed, having their way with the clothes of babes; of birds, massed, setting fires all over town. From the stage, over the choir and the orchestra, a shout rang out.

"Fire! Fire in the dome! Arsonists in the dome! Run for it!" I ran for it, all right. I flew for it. I got out my Dad's hole and, it being dark outside, clawed my way down to the ground.

Woodpecker feet are excellent for this kind of task and, unless you're an owl, you don't want to be flying around Tacoma (The City of High Voltage Lines) at night. The parking lot was quickly filled with human men running into that night, down onto the docks themselves. The fire engines were coming and I walked away, uptown, thinking, hopping, actually. I didn't smell any smoke. I hadn't seen any flames, except flames on film. Flames on film. Cameras. Hmmm.

Cameras and birds, I thought. Birds stole downtown? The pigeons and the gulls and the crows, even the woodpeckers? Why? To get the negatives away from E.Z. Haag? Because the negatives show birds dragging down the bridge? We are creatures of the wind, birds. I remembered that up on the screen were pictures of someone who looked for all the world like Frankie, of birds taking her clothes off. Did birds steal the downtown area as well as her clothes? If so, it was probably pigeons, but the plot could possibly include crows or ravens or thrushes or pee-wits. They stole pictures of Frankie, I was willing to bet, all of them. I looked in my wallet and, indeed, the picture of Frankie I'd had was gone. On the other hand, I was a bird, or something. We are the wind, we birds. I knew that and I'd probably packed the knowledge away for a rainy day, of which we have a few up here.

All birds know the story, one version of it or another. Should I tell the story to E.Z. Haag? Here's a scenario, I said to myself. Maybe E.Z. Haag's father had caught birds in action. Maybe the films showed birds dragging down the Galloping Gertie Bridge, birds dragging the halter tops off barely reluctant babes with breasts, birds in the depths of the night sky, winging across the moon, of birds as arsonists. Well, it was a thought. Birds, after all, are so much a part of the wind that they might as well be the wind itself. Certainly, we follow the wind's directions, we birds. Did arsonists? They, as well, I thought, are creatures of the wind, of the air itself. The Carbon Family, who ruled Tacoma's tawdry crime life in years past, were said to have once employed birds, even wood-peckers, as arsonists. There were whispers in the bird community, I'd heard them all my life. My Uncle's voice: "It's a fool of an arsonist, kid, who has to use a torch…" Wind, birds and arson. The City of Coinci-dence, the City of Conflagration. Fire burns the air. It was a thought.

I saw Frankie, then, under a streetlight. She was hanging out with some birds. The streetlight—like all the others in town—flashed blue and then went out. Sirens shrieked over the city. My heart was sus-pended somewhere between rising and sinking. There was flame in her hand as she lit a cigarette. The firelight showed her face for a moment and then she was gone.

Under the flickering streetlight, Frankie was hanging out with birds. I slowed down. I looked behind me. In front of me, there she was. She and her friends. Something was coming clear to me, but I wasn't sure what it was. There was a nighthawk with Frankie, a guy I'd seen around

Taco Town since I was a kid. Smartass. There was the usual collection of useless crows, cackling and clorking as if they had something really to talk about beyond their petty concerns. There was an owl or two. Night birds, you know the crowd. Jays with dark glasses. Birds smoking cigarettes. Crows: that pretty much says it all.

"Long time no see," I said to her because it was all I could think of to say. She was beautiful. I knew enough not to tell her she looked beautiful. She would have thought I was crazy. She thought I was crazy anyway.

"The whole point ," she said, peering at me, "the whole point is that we are married already. You seem to have conveniently forgotten that part, pal."

"Don't call me pal, honey," I whined. "You can't be that mad at me."

"I'm not mad at you, little buddy," she said, smoking her cigarette and looking imperious. "I've forgotten all about you, to tell you the truth. Ever since you forgot you married me…well, I've decided to just write you off. What an idiot you are. I can barely believe it. I've written you off, pal."

Chapter 6

I had to think about this. Were we really married? I stared up at her. She towered. I am a woodpecker, after all, and she is someone whose ancestors presumably evolved swinging from the low branches of savannah trees on a continent largely ignored by woodpeckers. They stretched, in other words. She was very tall, formidable you might say, but as beautiful certainly as any human or bird could be. There was just something about her. She got to me.

"C'mon, baby," I said plaintively.

The birds around her clucked and growled, not much singing, because it wasn't that time of year, of course. It sounded like they were laughing at me. They all lit up cigarettes.

"I don't get it," I said, lighting up a Lucky. "What do you care about the Keepers?" Silence all around. I winked at Frankie.

"Which one of you bastards hit me on the back of the head?" I asked.

"Fuck you, pal," laughed a blackbird. He lit up a big match for no reason at all and then blew it out. He laughed again, but this time it was an ominous laugh, "Either you're with us or you're against us, Woodpecker. And so far it's been looking like you're against us."

"That's why you conked me on the head? Because I'm not part of something I don't even know about?"

"Don't be naive, Woodpecker," said an owl. "We all know what we're talking about here, except maybe one or two of us who seem to think they're humans and not birds?" He stared pointedly at me. Then he turned his head completely around and looked pointedly behind him.

"I only hear rumors, I'm a little out of touch," I said as apologetically as possible. "It's not easy working among humans. After awhile you lose track of important events."

"I can understand that," said the owl. "Even now, things are going so slow it's driving me nutty." He whirled his head back around to the front.

"It's because of me, isn't it," said Frankie. "You all have to really slow down because of me being here, don't you? I suppose I should just leave," she sighed and blew cigarette smoke out in a big blue cloud.

They all chimed in; no, no, she shouldn't leave, don't be like that, Frankie, they said. We're only doing this because of you. And of course she stayed. I wasn't the only bird knocked out by Frankie, I remembered that she'd told me that she'd got interested in birds all of a sudden, maybe in her last year at Stadium High School, and she started looking at birds, then feeding birds, read a couple of Roger Tory Peterson field guides and evidently married me, a bird. She was a quick study. She wasn't that far out of high school, anyway. She was a baby, really, in human terms. By birds' standards, she was ancient, of course.

"Let's be frank here—sorry, Frankie," said one of the hawks in a gentlemanly manner. "All I mean is, we're talking about some kind of essence here, the essence of inter-species activity perhaps. Bird-human marriages—I know it's a delicate issue—well, they seem downright bizarre to a lot of people and worse to most birds."

"Damn straight," said Frankie, somewhat defensively it seemed to me. She still looked beautiful. We were all smoking now. Sirens wailed around us but no flames shot up into the night air above the docks. No weird or flickering shadows spread out from the dark figures of any of the fleeing humans or standing birds. There were no flames at all, in point of fact.

"Hey, look," said the nighthawk, blinking furiously, "I personally don't care, I mean it's all right with me. Whatever. I just mean that a lot of people find it…you know, a somewhat difficult issue to deal with. Directly."

"Well," I said. "Okay, I see what you mean. Look, I'm probably at fault here. Okay, so there may be something in the idea that Frankie and I are already married. It probably happened pretty quickly, see? You have to understand that, sweet as she is, she doesn't really comprehend the huge metabolic differences between Avian-Americans and so-called humans."

Frankie raised her big eyes to the night stars and sighed loudly. A couple of her bird buddies laughed sympathetically.

"Okay, I'm probably entirely at fault," I whined, like the sapsucker I am. "I admit I got fascinated with humans when I was little. It was obviously because my Dad spent so much time with them down in Hollywood. It was natural that I would be interested and want to know more." I wanted her back, this much was clear. Snickers ran through the little group like candy bars running around the ankles of adult humans.

"Look," I said. "I'm probably the only one here who makes an actual living in the human world. You don't have to tell me the problems involved. It's true; you've got to slow down some, to be sure. Even then, humans seem laconic, at best, to most birds. I know this. It may be the reason humans seem to live a long time, that's what birds think, for the most part, am I right?" They mostly nodded yes. The way I try to explain it, if anyone (like Frankie, for instance) were ever interested, is that birds download information in much the same way that digital information is downloaded over the short-wave bands of the human radio. All a human hears is a burst of noise (I'm guessing here), but with the same information, at a much different time scale, birds are hearing—seeing—the equivalent of, say, the Library at Alexandria. For instance, the songs of birds must be slowed down, way down, to have even a hope of the studied understanding or attention of humans and bird songs are the least complicated of bird utterances, of bird downloadings.

"What about the Mob?" I asked. "Is that what this is all about really?"

"We're not a fucking mob, pal," said a hummingbird, a tough little sonofabitch with a lot of rufous and iridescence. I'd seen the type. These are the kind of wise guys who regularly grab sap from a sapsucker's legitimate workplace. They think they're smart because they're so small.

"What the hell are you thinking about?" snarled the little bastard.

"Aren't crows prone to mobbing?" I asked more calmly than I felt. I lit up another Lucky. A lot of corvid activity is bizarre by anyone's standards, so I felt I was on semi-safe ground. For instance, stuffing pine nuts in holes already pecked by hard-working woodpeckers might be equated with banking; that is, putting things of value in holes that others have labored years to produce and taking an extraordinary profit for it, gaining power by exploiting the honest efforts of others. You were always pretty safe going after the tattered reputations of crows.

"We're ravens," said the two big guys (or girls, it's impossible to tell with ravens and they'll tell you much the same story). "Mobbing is for amateurs who have problems with hawks. We don't have any problems with hawks now, do we?" They looked archly over at three hawks in the shadows. They were blinking. Hawks don't like nighttime, except for nighthawks, of course and even the one nighthawk had on dark glasses: French ones, if I'm any judge.

"Is this about the bridge?" I finally asked. "Is this about the bridge falling down or not really falling down and downtown disappearing or not really, and the strange mist and a robbery downtown from a place called the Eye Shoppe?" They all looked guilty as hell, except Frankie. She always gets that kind of wide-eyed look when she realizes that I'm a lot more on top of things than she ever thinks I am. I tried to laugh, but I have to admit that I was pretty damn nervous. A mist had begun to seep in around us.

The hummingbird had a gun. It was a little gun, but I'm a little guy. I grabbed Frankie and ran for it. She had on high heels and I had to reach up to grab her hand, but she went with me, which surprised me. I wanted to fly, even at night, but I knew I couldn't drag Frankie up there with me.

"C'mon, baby," I growled. "Keep up with me."

"Oh, Ed," she whined plaintively, "Don't drag me. Don't run away from me. Don't fly, please don't fly off and leave me again. I love you."

That stopped me. She loved me. Me. A woodpecker. Me, a Wood-pecker. My heart went all gooey, as gooey as a melted Brown and Haley (Makes 'em Daily) Candy. I pulled her into an abandoned doorway in the old Brown and Haley (makes 'em daily) Candy factory. The smell of chocolate and pecans was all around us. The mist was all around us too. It was thick and getting thicker, wet and getting gooey. It began to swirl around her little pumps and she stood up on her tippy-toes and she looked so cute that I had to grab her around the knees and just give her a hug.

"Married or not, babe, hitched or unhitched," I gabbled, "I love you. You've got to believe that."

"Love isn't everything, Ed," she said, looking down at me with what seemed to be little droplet tears in her big eyes. "A lot of people think love is everything, and I suppose it is to them, but to me it isn't, see? I think there are higher standards and I'm going to try to hew to them instead of just wasting my life on someone I love."

"You love me. You said it again."

"Of course I do," she said. The mist was up to her waist now which meant that all she could see of me was my hat. "Of course I love you, you stupid woodpecker. I loved you from the first minute I saw you. There's something about you that just makes a gal like me want to go down to the Thriftway and buy some birdseed." This, of course, was one of our problems. She insisted on thinking that I liked birdseed, which is only nominally true. I prefer insects, grubs and a nice single cheeseburger with onions from the Frisko Freeze, to tell you the truth, but I never had the guts to tell her that. Maybe that's one reason I'd forgotten we were married. Too much birdseed. I had to sneak it away and give it to titmice down at the Titmouse Shelter on Division Avenue so she'd think I was just gobbling it up.

Footsteps in the mist. A streetlamp trying to cut through. The shadow on the shattered bricks. The sounds of breathing, mine and hers.

A bullet floated down the alleyway in slow motion, spinning slowly and looking for me. It cut a long funnel through the mist. I pulled Frankie down into the thick stuff as it shot past, it didn't make a sound. From far away, you could hear the bang from the gun. That was a fast bullet, I thought.

Running, pulling. Why do babes always keep their high heels on at times like this? C'mon. Panting. Into another doorway. Breathing. Listening. My gun is out. I have a gun.

"Honey," she whispered. "Honey, this is stupid. It doesn't even seem vaguely real."

Another bullet came twisting through the fog, searching down the brick tunnel. It smashed flat on a brick. Far away, I could hear the blast.

"Not real? Are you crazy? What did you think *that* was?"

"What was what?" she asked. Omigod, I realized. The bullet had been moving so fast that she didn't even see it. Why were we still talking and seeing each other if the outside world seemed to be switching on and off between bird time and human time? Was this love?

"You tell me. Is it love? Is that why you don't see the bullets?" I tried to keep my voice down.

"Yes," she said firmly, as if we were now getting to the actual point of a discussion. "I've never understood why you seem so dense on the subject. Love is a place of absolute safety and infinite hope. I love you. You love me. What bullets?"

Chapter 7

One of the things I like most about being a detective is freedom from the kind of pointless ambiguity that practically overwhelms most people. When you're a detective, you take on a case and the case—just by virtue of being a case—has an end and that's because it either comes to a solid, non-ambiguous solution or because whoever was paying you just isn't paying you anymore. So, you walk away. You are neither judge nor jury. You've done your job. You're just the detective. Walk away. Fly away. A lot of people—even a lot of birds—might consider my attitude hard-boiled, but you have to remember that any bird will inevitably have profoundly mixed feelings about the concept of hard-boiling anything, even thoughts. This case wasn't over, that much I knew. My wallet (I have a wallet) was still full.

Frankie and I were breathing hard, but we seemed to be alive, if not exactly safe. There were no bullets anymore. We had determined we were in love. How bad could it be? The fog lifted a bit and you could see the little lights of Gig Harbor out across the great bay. It seemed to be getting hot again, even though it was night. I felt positively human. I reached up and took Frankie's hand and told her I agreed with her about anything she might think or say and she laughed at me in a nice enough way and we crept in the overshadows of the scalloped awnings up Pacific Avenue, right into downtown Tacoma, right to the Eye Shoppe and there was light there and inside was E.Z. Haag, working late, talking on the telephone.

"I'm on the phone to my little sister down in California," he said as he let us in. "She thinks it's peculiar that I've hired a woodpecker."

"People in California are so peculiar they've lost all perspective on what peculiar actually is," I said reassuringly.

Frankie looked up at the tall walls. "Hey. What happened to that big picture of me that used to hang up there?" she demanded.

"They stole everything, I told you, baby," I said.

"They're stealing pictures of me? That isn't good." She was in what I like to describe as a state of flounce.

"You're right," I said. "In fact, they even got the picture of you I carry around in my wallet."

"Well, that's all right," she said, looking for an ashtray and a place high enough to sit so she could cross her legs correctly. "I hated that picture," she said, lighting up a Lucky. E.Z. Haag hung up the phone and twisted the top off a beer with "Ice" in its name. He drank and then he surveyed us.

"Once this town was the Hub of Northwest Industry," said E.Z. Haag. "We were a Place to Learn, a Place to Live, a Place to Relax, Play and Shop. Best of all, we were a place where the goddamn Eye Shoppe made money year after god damn year." He paused. "And then there was nothing," he said softly, but not so softly we couldn't hear. "And then we were no more. You'd have thought the Mountain had erupted and wiped us all out. What's up, Ed?" He looked at me searchingly. "Turned anything up?"

"Here's the deal, E.Z.," I said, as gently as I could, "and it's not a good deal, as far as I can tell. We're in a weird place."

"You don't have to tell me that. This town used to be Beautiful, Progressive, Convenient and Inviting," said E.Z. Haag with some emphasis. "Now it's just weird. I used to enjoy my work. I used to want to work twenty-some hours a day. Now all I want to do is sleep. In this town, We Liked You and We Knew You'd Like Us. We Were the Place to Visit."

"We were the City of Chrysanthemums," said Frankie helpfully.

"We were Interesting," said Ed, encouraged. "We were the Nerve Center for the County, we were just a Bridge Crossing from Gig Harbor (Land of Intrigue and Quiet Beauty), we had a Heritage we would Long Wish to Remember, we were the possessors of the Third Longest Suspension Bridge in the World..."

"Until the fucking thing fell down," Frankie interjected softly.

Both E.Z. Haag and I looked at her. "Where did you hear that?" we both said, practically at the same time.

"It's common knowledge," said Frankie, although she seemed a little flustered.

"No, it isn't," said the big man. He looked suspicious. He looked over at me. "It isn't. Not among humans, it isn't."

"I didn't say a thing to her," I said.

"He never tells me anything," complained Frankie. "It wasn't him that told me, anyway. You can believe that. No, it's common knowledge among..."

"Who? Birds?" he asked.

"You see," I tried to shut her up, "I've had a kind of revelation, a kind of human shoring-up of something birds pretty much take for granted. It's good for me, if you see what I mean."

"I don't care what you mean," said E.Z. Haag evenly. "And I don't care what's good for you. I'm beginning to get suspicious."

I probably shouldn't have, but I told him the easy part, how I had figured out that there were two different times operating in Tacoma—the City Out of Joint—and that therefore Tacoma-in-Washington-State should properly be likened to the Mystery-Spot-in-California, or the innumerable attractions like it: the Whirlpool-of-the-Woods or the Elves-on-a-Spot or The Mystery Tree or the Goofy House in Pucay, Indiana. Tacoma—in the State of Washington—just had some Time anomaly going for it, perhaps some random fluctuation of the magnetosphere, perhaps some unimagined—even by birds—symmetry.

"You're about as crazy as a hoot owl, Ed," said E.Z. Haag.

"No, I'm not," I said. "And technically, there is no such thing as a hoot owl."

"I know that," he said testily. "It's a kind of figure of speech."

"Don't try to confuse me," I said.

"Birds," said E.Z. Haag. "I knew it. What is it with you, Ed? Were you lying to me when you said you didn't know about the bridge going down?"

"No," I said. "I live in both worlds. Sometimes it takes me a while to catch up in one or the other." I tried to be gentle with Frankie. "Was it that bunch you were with under the streetlamp? Did they tell you about the bridge?"

Frankie looked guilty. "I'm not supposed to say."

So the old stories were true, I thought. The old Tacoma bird stories about arson and the wind and the big war and the welds that sank the ships, the bad welds by birds that dropped the old iron bridge into the drink. Birds don't understand humans well and birds in Tacoma have always wondered if the humans knew the same story. I knew they didn't. Maybe I was the only bird who did.

E.Z. Haag looked troubled. "I used to have pictures of birds pulling on the bridge, of birds making the bridge fall down. I used to have pictures of birds with torches talking to Carbons. I used to have the whole story. And then the birds got the negatives. You're just fronting for them, Ed."

"Then why did you hire me?" I wanted to keep him talking. He had that crazy look in his eye that guys in his position in the movies get when the movie gets to this point. He looked nuts and talkative, in other words. He would tell me anything because he was going to kill me, that sort of thing.

"Look, E.Z.," I babbled. "From what I can see, there are two times operating here. Let's call them bird time and human time."

"Let's," chirped Frankie cheerfully.

"Now in one or the other—say in bird time in Tacoma—bullets are flying and synchronies of birds and bridges are wreaking havoc and at the same place, there's also human time in Tacoma, and that's where things are disappearing and reappearing in a seemingly random manner—random unless you count the kind of human who might try to manipulate the situation."

"You're saying my photographs and equipment and negatives have been randomly manipulated?"

"Did I say randomly?" We stared at each other. This involved me turning sideways. He looked guilty enough for both of us.

"I know you've still got the negatives, E.Z." I ventured. "It's easy enough to pretend to clean out your own store. I know something else, too, that you've been holding the bridge collapse pictures so that you might blackmail the town. If the town finds out the bridge collapsed years ago, then they'd have to ask some real tough questions about the facts of their own existence. Every Tacoman thinks he's been over that bridge and if it wasn't there, then *where is he*? See? It's existential, practically. I wouldn't be surprised if you had pictures of birds committing arson and worse. You want to blame something on the birds in order to protect yourself."

"I'm confused," said Frankie, vaguely. "I wonder if it's too late to go see a movie."

"Well, the birds *are* guilty, Ed. You know that as well as I do. You know the story, don't you?" E.Z. Haag was looking shiftily around. I wondered if he had a gun.

"How did you find out there *was* a story?"

"A little bird told me."

"A pee-wit? An Empidonax Flycatcher?"

"How would I know?"

"You seem to have your methods."

"So do you. And your methods seem to have turned up nothing. I heard you were with the cops at the dome tonight."

"If you've heard that, you've been talking to the cops. Were those all cops in the dome, all of them?"

"Didn't you figure that out, Woodpecker? Of course they are. Some of them are honorary cops, but a cop is a cop. It was a Keepers meeting to talk about the mobbing. Mobbing, get what I mean? And Woodpecker, it seems to me that you're the head of the whole damn mobbing plot. A guy like you thinks he can come into a town like this and just marry a little gal who's…who's…"

Omigod, I thought. Now I get it. Of course, this guy used to have Frankie's picture up in his store. He was the only person close enough to me today to get into my wallet and grab her picture from there. Yeah, my wallet usually lies out, I probably left it in the reception room. This guy's in love with Frankie, I thought.

"You're in love with me, aren't you," asked Frankie. She tried to make the stool she was perched on twirl, but it wouldn't. "I remember you.

You were a senior at Staydumb High School when I was a freshman. You were considered quite a catch."

"Someone caught me. I'm still caught, more's the pity. But now all that's going to change." He looked at her with a deep look in his eyes.

E.Z. Haag had a gun, it turned out, a little nine mil Glock but it was enough to kill a woodpecker. He pulled it out of his shoe and laid it on the empty counter and looked solemnly at it.

"You may very well be right about the time anomaly, Ed," he said. "I hadn't thought of it, frankly."

"Frankie," said Frankie. "My name's Frankie." She was nervous, I could tell.

"Your picture used to hang right up there. I'm in love with you, baby, and so are half the guys who used to make up Downtown Tacoma."

"Yes, of course," said Frankie, staring at the gun. "Yes."

He picked up the pistol and pointed it at me. "Ed, now that you've made an investigation, I realize that the birds don't have a clue what I'm doing. I had to find out. I used a bird to get to the birds."

I jumped him then. I had to. It's traditional. I flew straight at him. This confuses humans, I've generally found and it certainly did in this case. Instead of firing the gun, he shrieked and covered his head with his arms. I grabbed his gun and threw it as far away as I could. I pulled my own .38 and held it on him and pulled Frankie behind me and we got the hell out of there.

Chapter 8

Frankie had a convertible and she seemed to have no trouble at all getting it started. She fired it down Pacific Avenue through Tacoma at night. We sped down Jackson and hurled ourselves out onto the Galloping Gertie Bridge as it began to sway ominously in the night wind, twisted by one of those erratic blows from the South that make the big monstrosity sway and buckle. The huge green old thing was stretched out across the dangerous water, its thin thread of a roadway pulled up twice by tall vertical towers made of ancient metals and chemistry which crossers-over are assured are stable enough but which may not be. On this night, some few cars whirred over the modern grid of asphalt on steel. The pavement hummed. The little lights shone. The clock ticked, and then they were gone. She stopped the convertible in the middle of the span and after awhile, no other cars came across. The bridge began to sway and twist. It creaked and groaned. Above us, cables snapped like gunshots.

"Why in God's name are you a detective?" Frankie asked me suddenly, coolly. The convertible was in neutral with the engine running still. She had thrown a bandanna with pictures of cowboys on it over her head and tied it under her chin.

"I don't know, really." I said. "Drive on. Let's get out of here."

"What are you nervous about?" she asked gaily.

"I'm not exactly nervous," I said. I wasn't nervous because I knew I could fly. Nothing could happen on a bridge that I couldn't handle. In fact, when you think about it, a bridge is a clumsy kind of flight. It's a suspension, in other words. If I was nervous, it was because I didn't see any way I could save her if the bridge went down.

"Why are you a detective?" she asked again.

"I suppose being a detective has basically something to do with asking questions."

"That's the truth. You got that right," she said. "Detectives are trying to figure something out," she said, "if you really want to simplify it. So love," she said, "is a mixed blessing, huh? In other words, the detective's best friend," she said, "is also the detective's worst enemy. You can't figure love out, right?"

"Well, right," I said. "Just don't forget anger and recrimination and bullets here and there and now and again and as well the hot kiss at the end of a wet fist sometimes," I said. "Some people are in detection for the action. Some people are in it for the money. No one's in it for love." She laughed at the idea of me making any money from detecting. She kept the books at Ed Woodpecker, P.I., after all.

"Well, yes," she said. "But love is bigger than murder, if you're feeling it, if you're in love, isn't that true?"

The bridge nearly turned over. I figured honesty might make her drive on. If the bridge collapsed, she would die because one measly woodpecker wasn't strong enough to save her from falling. "I can't imagine love and murder in the same room," I said, hoping that would please her.

She turned off the engine. It was dead silent except for the occasional crack of a cable bursting and the howling of the wind as it rocked the great, green bridge and it twisted underneath us.

"Right!" she shouted earnestly. "That's what I mean! If there's murder in the room, there's no love and if there's love in the room, no murder."

"Not in any room in Tacoma. Not that I've seen." I tried not to panic, but I got myself perched up on the seatback just in case.

Her eyes were big. "Love is bigger than questions or rape and bigger than corruption and hypocrisy, bigger than incest and rage, bigger than evil, bigger than money, bigger than…everything. Love is trust."

I couldn't argue with her. She was saying that love—of all things—was what our—hers and mine—what our whole story was about; that our—hers and my—story might have been some kind of adventure, might have been some literate conventional detective story with the chattered shadow of the Venetian blind across the arching black panther ashtray, the syringe nearby, or the blue steel gun with smoke threading from its hot barrel. Instead, this story turned out to be about love, pure and simple. And it was therefore a story about eternal love, because that's what Frankie and I are all about, whatever you might think about it. The fact that I am a bird and she a human has nothing to do with eternal love, it turns out. Or everything to do with it.

I noticed birds on the bridge, a mob of birds, by the looks of things. Then the bridge fell. It heaved and it cracked and it twisted itself loose from whatever great suspension held it there. With a scream, the great mob of birds lifted off and made a split-second decision and all turned at once and all flew to the spot in the air where Frankie hung suspended, the convertible falling beneath her, where she hung before the falling that would lead to her certain death on the black water beneath. Her eyes locked with mine. I tried to grab her as she dropped, but then the mob swarmed over me and got under her and nicely pushed her out of the way of the crumbling tower and then bounced her two or three times in the sucking air and pushed her out of its whirlpool of death and then bounced her down to the shore and eventual safety.

Through it all, she had only looked into my eyes and smiled and smiled. I guess her point was that there had been nothing to be frightened of all along, but I was still scared to death. I'd nearly lost her. She was safe. She'd made friends in both worlds and now I could see why.

"A bridge is a suspension. *It is a kind of flight.* Maybe there's some secret in this," she shouted at me, as I flew straight up, laughing and crying. I'd had it with my life, that much I knew. There had to be more to life than just asking a lot of questions.

Today I caught a heck of a nice Carpenter Ant out over the Nisqually Basin while doing a little surveillance on Grape Island for a new client. I like Carpenter ants and hadn't had one in years, not since the family used to camp out in the Mystery Island cedars when my Dad wasn't working so much down in California. I'm trying to get out of the office and do a few more bird things lately, I swear. I met a nice girl, a bird in fact, in fact a woodpecker from that bunch over on Mystery Island and it turns out she's quite interested in detection and humans in a general kind of way. But Frankie's come back to work now, so she doesn't really stand a chance.

Frankie sits outside my office with her legs crossed and her nylons straight and she reads detective magazines and does her nails under the yellowed light of a copper lamp shaped like a fish with an amber lampshade on its head. Inside my office, I yearn for her, even though she's just outside.

"Tacoma," Frankie said once, long ago, "is a mysterious place, and that's about all there is to it."

That isn't all there is to it, of course, but it's nice she thinks so.

THE
REGIONAL

AMERICAN
SURREALIST
Cookbook

The Northeast

This is a strange area of the country, its cuisine matching its clam rivers and mystic flattened foods.

COOKING SHOW SOUFFLÉ
Submitted by: Martha Stewart of New York City,
New York
   "This is an excellent recipe. Although it
   requires quite a bit more time than I'd
   originally bargained for."

Serves 6
Preparation time: 3 years

INGREDIENTS:
1 TV crew
12 dozen chicken eggs, beaten
1 truckload of milk
16 cases of butter
2 stoves
1 contract, drained
3 publicists, crushed
½ tsp. salt
6 weeping assistants
Storyboards
1 phone call
Jail time

Preheat one oven to 325 degrees F. Pretend to
preheat the other. Attend endless meetings.
Grease 15 casserole dishes. Berate assistants.
Place a layer of crushed eggshells in the bottom
of 1 garbage can. Layer garbage neatly. Receive
phone calls. Make phone calls. Get up early. Be
driven. Get script. Make revisions. Practice
smiling. Make assistants cry. Add butter, 1 tsp.
Go to jail. Reinvent self. Start another
magazine. Receive plaudits of employees. Go to
work every day. Try not to be too lonely.
Assistants weep in the hallway.

SHROUDED CHICKEN
Submitted by: Gwang Ho of Never, New Jersey
   "Not wishing to quite far. So being so. It can
   be said."

Serves 200
Preparation time: Not so bad, considering

INGREDIENTS:
A whole bunch of chickens
200 little outfits (sailor, ballerina, etc.)
A lot of packaged stuffing mix
A real big plate or platter (platelet will not do)
Small coffins

Dress chickens in little outfits. Prepare
stuffing per package instructions. Boil or fry
the chickens, it hardly matters which. Stuff
cavities, including pockets in outfits. Prepare
individual coffins, reserving about 20 for ashes
later. Scorch about 20 chickens. Reserve ashes.
Serve with funereal music. Sprinkle ashes on top.

The Midwest

*Perhaps the most normal-appearing section
of the country, this flat land, with its rivers lower and
its cities higher, still manages to produce some of the food we fear most.*

SLICER-DICER MELANGE
Submitted by: R. Popeil of Chicago, Illinois
   "But wait, there's more..."

Preparation time: 1 crazy moment

INGREDIENTS:
1 murdered husband
1 remarriage
2 cases of tomatoes
Case of onions
1 tsp. vinegar
1 hands-free microphone
1 amplifier
1 tsp. salt
Red pepper
Closet

Whisk microphone and amplifier until fluffed.
Combine tomatoes and onions. Invent scalp-dye
with vinegar and pepper. Hide. In a medium bowl
talk quickly and convincingly. Hope for the best.

FESTIVE HOLIDAY BULIMIC TURKEY
Submitted by: Unnamed of Edge of Nowhere, Indiana
   "I don't care what they think! It's just eat,
   eat, eat! Disgusting!"

Preparation time: It sneaks up on you...

INGREDIENTS:
1 small turkey
2 fingers
A toilet bowl

Leave nothing to the imagination, leave nothing on the tiles, leave nothing that would create a trail back to you. Leave early, claiming some emergency or other.

HURLED EGGS
Submitted by: Tandom Koolzip of Peeorhea, Indianolapolis
  "This is a recipe that was tossed to me by someone claiming to be my grandmother."

Preparation time: Instantaneous

INGREDIENTS:
Eggs
Someone to throw eggs at

That's all she wrote.

KANSAS CITY OYSTERS
Submitted by: Big "Chief"
Tom of Kansas City, Kansas

INGREDIENTS:
Cab fare
1 doz. oysters
1 gal. bourbon whiskey

Get oysters drunk on whiskey. Put them in a cab. Give driver cab fare and tell him to take them to Kansas City.

The Southwest

The sound of cars in the night, the long trail of asphalt, writing things down on long rolls of waxed paper on top of small refrigerators...

ROAD CHICKEN
Submitted by: Dean Moriarty of Denver, Colorado
  "Man, I gotta get me some coffee. We gotta stop soon, man. What was that? Did you feel that?"

Preparation time: 10 minutes, at most

INGREDIENTS:
Road something   2 tsp. pine nuts
1 cup bread tips   2 cans corn niblets
1 lb. tater tots   An Unformed Being
Weed (Roaster)   Backseat ashes

Throw things around. Add things. Drink alcohol.
Smoke. You've crossed that intersection for the
last time.

ORANGE PORK
Submitted by: Juan Guadalupe
of Quitobaquito, Arizona
  "Park and Lock it. Not responsible."

INGREDIENTS:
Crate of oranges   1 gun
1 Javelina   Full moon

Do the math.

The West Coast

The perfectly possible is always near. This region, though largely ignored, is full of food.

1955 PIE
Submitted by: Elmer Batters of Hollywood,
California
  "I'm probably dead, but you wouldn't know it to
  look at me."

Preparation time: Dreaming and drifting away

INGREDIENTS:
2 plastic, see-through, 5-inch tall high heels
Flouncy apron with clever sayings
Pink frilled trim (for apron)
Several pies, lattice-top and otherwise
A garage
Rope   Bangs
A corset   A dim red light

Elude capture. Stand for hours in darkrooms with
red light. Ignore greenhouse gases. Ignore
deposits. Ignore erosion and gross inadequacies,
stubbornness and melted polar ice. Bring
ingredients to a boil. Serve 3 degrees hotter
than ever before.

URINATED CHICKEN
Submitted by: Andrew Wamasake of Gardena,
California

Preparation time: Maybe 5 hours

INGREDIENTS:
One chicken
A lot of water
Large drinking glass

Run chicken around and take its temperature. Give
the chicken a couple of options. Leave chicken
alone a lot. Make sure chicken has a lot of water
in its bowl.

The South

*A puzzling region, given to elaborate eccentricities and bizarre memories.
It's a good place for surreal juxtapositions.*

GLAMOROUS FISH
Submitted by: Horton Capote of Asheville, North or
South Carolina
  "I'm so delighted with myself, just so delighted
  with myself."

INGREDIENTS:
Beauty products
Thick Italian magazines
Fish

REENACTMENT CASSEROLE
Submitted by: Kenneth Burns of Public, Florida
  "I think vignettes are good, are pure and
  simple. I like fine sound editing."

Preparation time: Hundreds of years

INGREDIENTS:
A Civil War
Blowing clouds
¼ cup banjo music
Peck of voice-overs
12 t. suspenders
Dark shoes of all sizes
2 cups body makeup
Blood (chocolate syrup may be substituted)
Alligators (crocodiles may be substituted)
Guns

Whip clouds to a froth. Reserve 1/3 cup of
voice-overs. Spread music over top.

REPUBLICAN CABLEHAIR CORDON PREMIER
Submitted by: Annie Coulter of Foxnews, Georgia
  "I wish nothing but ill on liberals. I loathe
  them."

INGREDIENTS:
1 tbsp. plus 2 tsp. acerbic acid
1 clove reason, peeled and forced
¼ teaspoon each dried and finely pursed lips and
  knees
Grated peel of 1 psyche
2 whole breasts, exposed toward the top
2 paper-thin brain slices

Prepare an herbed compote of confused leanings.
Baffle liberal parents. Ignore insufficient
boyfriend. Keep it up.

DEAD RABBIT

INGREDIENTS:
Time
A rabbit

Porky Pika and the Search for the Missing Star

✿

When it gets right down to it, the best stories are the ones we tell when falling asleep in a tent on nights underneath so many stars as to strain the eye of man and beast. These stories have few rules, the primary one being that all animals should have last names that start with the same letter as their first. This story is one of Oona's favorites and I'll try to tell it to you as I did to her one night after dinner and a campfire up in the Four Jeffrey Campground at about eight thousand feet in the Eastern Sierras, just under the fourteen thousand feet peaks and far above the High Desert of the Great Basin to the east.

"You better tell me a story now," she'll say, once we're settled and snuggled in. She brings a sea of pillows on a car-camping trip like this and our nylon tent is big enough for a tall person like her to stand straight up in. We had five dogs then and they are asleep all around and on top of our down sleeping bags with us inside.

"I don't know any stories," I'll say. "I've used them all up. I've told you a story every night of this trip and you've done basically nothing."

"Don't be stupid. I do everything for you. What's the story?"

I'll think for a minute and remember the marmots and ground squirrels and pikas, all the industrious meadow and rock habitants of our daylight hikes and I'll take a breath and hope I come up with something good.

"Okay," I'll say, starting in. "Okay...uh, Porky and Petunia Pika live on Pika's Peak which is a high mountain in the Eastern Sierras of California."

"Please," she says sarcastically. "You're saying that Porky and Petunia are not pigs, but pikas?"

"Their parents were fond of old Warner Brothers cartoons," I say defensively.

"You're running low on material. This better be good."

You can tell where pikas live because their urine drippings show white on the huge granite boulders, so they're hard to miss, to say the least. Porky and Petunia were in the haying business, cutting grass in their mountain meadows and drying and storing it away in Porky's barn. Porky had a T-bird, a rare and restored '58 with original upholstery and engine package which he liked to drive slowly around the North Lake road because to drive it fast would be to kick up a lot of white, sticky granite dust and it takes a small animal like a pika a week or more to clean a Thunderbird, time a pika dare not waste during haying season. He made the car pay for itself though, because he would occasionally hire it out to some rich pikas over at North Lake, many of whom were Petunia's relatives.

Now this story truly starts on the momentous day when Porky and Petunia had a big party to celebrate the near end of haying season and a guy came to the party who was named Sherman Shrew, a little guy, as are all shrews. Sherman had a pole and a bandanna which certainly qualified him as a hobo or at least a hobo impersonator and as well, he wanted a job. Porky had no work for any shrew but recommended that Sherm ask over at that railroad that Mortimer Mouse had made in a tunnel that stretched from the Eastern Sierra clear to Denver, over in Colorado. Porky had once traveled all the way to Denver to visit his friend Kevin. It takes three years one way and three years back. It's quite an investment in time, in other words.

"What is the name of the railroad?" She doesn't sound at all asleep yet.

"It's called the Bishop, Tonopah and Pacific Railroad."

"I thought you said it went to Denver, not to the Pacific."

"Oh. Maybe it was the Denver, Tonopah and Pacific with a stop up in the mountains above Bishop."

"That makes some kind of sense," she says kindly enough.

Porky pointed out that from the way Sherman looked he might be able to get a job on the railroad as a hobo entertainer because Porky watched a lot of television and some of his favorite programs were those shows on public broadcasting about clever entertainment train trips with storytellers and banjo players.

"Kill me, kill me now," she moans.

"Well, look, Sherman needed a job. Shrewing wasn't going well and he was single and alone. Anyway that's exactly what happened. He got hired on and he rode the train east, playing the banjo and pretending to be a hobo. One night, in the bar of the sky car, he met Sherry Shrew, a smallish girl from Fort Dodge, Kansas who did nails right up until the time that all the cute names for nail salons got used up."

"Do shrews have to cut their nails before they grow too long?" she asks.

"Exactly," I say. "Oddly enough, that's how they started talking."

Sherry had asked Sherman about his nails, which looked pretty good by her somewhat exacting standards. And he told her that at eleven thousand feet in the Sierras, your nails get worn down without having to go to a nail salon, as opposed to shrews who lived in places like Denver or Fort Dodge, Kansas, where there are no abrasive rocks to speak of.

"There is not rock one in all Kansas," said Sherry. "And that's the God's truth."

She was out of cigarettes and Sherman ordered up two more highballs and a pack of Tareytons. Mortimer Mouse was good to his employees and had paid Sherman in advance for the first week so Sherman could afford it. He and Sherry were alone except for a bored bartender. Above them, above the great dome of the Observation Car, the stars were so many as to be uncountable. The train plunged into yet another tunnel. The entire three-year trip involved mostly tunnels, because the

Denver, Fort Dodge and Pacific Railroad was tiny and largely underground having been built by small burrowing animals for the most part.

"Don't ask," I say. "Fort Dodge is right next to Tonopah, Nevada, as the crow flies."

"And how does that crow fly?" she laughs.

"Low and slow, babe," I say. "Aren't you asleep yet?"

"Who could sleep listening to something as fascinating as this?" I laugh. "What was the bartender's name?"

"He didn't have a name," I say quickly. "Mortimer Mouse insisted on it. Animals had evidently run out of alphabet."

"Similar to that nail salon problem," she says.

Meanwhile (an excellent word when telling a story) back at Pika's Peak, Porky and Petunia's neighbors were spending more time around Porky and Petunia what with haying season coming to an end. Bancroft and Betty Belding, a couple of ground squirrels who enjoyed standing up on their hind legs and chattering at the top of their lungs like crazy people, lived just down the hill. Bancroft owned some kind of bizarre squirrel bank that moved from place to place everyday and randomly forgot where its depositors had their deposits but he had once been President of All Ground Squirrels. Betty was well-liked, but developed a fungal abuse problem which she kicked and then wrote a book and eventually founded the Betty Belding Clinic which met with great success.

Another neighbor was Marty Marmot who lived on the North Lake road with many of his relatives: hundreds of them, in fact. Marty had a scientific and intellectual bent. He had graduated from the University of the Pacific down in the Valley in Stockton on the far west side of the Sierras. His wife Maureen Marmot was a book illustrator. Porky stopped to talk to Marty one day, leaving the motor running on the T-Bird and leaning out the window.

"How's it goin'?" said Marty.

"Same ol', same ol'," said Porky. "Workin' hard?"

"Hardly workin'," laughed Marty. This was the way people talked on Pika's Peak and they enjoyed doing it.

"You got *that* right," said Porky.

Marty had grown up on the North Lake road. He went to college and got two advanced degrees in Marmot Studies and met Maureen Marmot there. They married and then he wrote *The Book of Marmots* which

Maureen illustrated and they made a lot of money and then came back home to the North Lake road to retire.

So one day Marty and Bancroft went over to Porky's barn. Porky could only be talked to through a small window in the rock because of his fear of wolverines. The rock was pretty much the roof of the haying barn. Porky would sit in his little office made of hay and watch TV and he could only get Nickelodeon and the Cartoon Network on the cable system that serviced small animals at great heights. He particularly liked the cartoon called *Hey, Arnold* and could hum the theme song all the way through, snapping his stubby Pika fingers at the right times. As haying season closed down and fall loomed over the meadows and rocks and crevices of the hillside, Porky and Petunia used to drag out the hay cart and service the surrounding populace with the popular attraction called Porky's Hayrides in which Porky would hook up the T-Bird to the haying cart and make the grand circle around North Lake, slowly so as not to kick up dust.

On one of these moonlit rides, Porky and Petunia discovered that one star was missing. Petunia was the one who noticed actually. She was sitting up in the hay wagon with the customers as Porky was driving the T-Bird around the lake. The customers were ooohing and aahing over the stars, lying back in the new-mown hay. They were mostly chickarees that night, so there was the usual amount of aimless chatter and Betty had enough time to look up at the sky.

The search for the missing star. They searched for six years. Then Sherman and Sherry Shrew came back on the train and they had found the missing star. It had been in the observation car the whole time.

"Are you asleep?" I whisper. No answer comes. She looks as pretty as ever. One of our many dogs has draped a doggie foot across her head. There's no need for a moon outside, because the stars are all out, all of them. Not one is missing.

X Is for Christmas
A Tale of the Old Detective

✧

"It's a mystery, Christmas, that's what it is," the Old Detective grumbled. "There's no mystery to Hanukkah, for instance. After all, it's a celebration tailor-made for creatures of the desert and Jews, for all their intelligence, are not a basically ironic people. But Christmas in Hollywood is a kind of puzzle, you've got to admit, especially for someone from a more northern climate."

The old man and I were sitting in a little bar on Hollywood Boulevard, one he had liked to frequent in older, more violent days, when dolls and sharpies ruled the boulevard. It was the day before the day that even down here in the chaparral we like to call Christmas. The bar was called the Blue Mechanism, for reasons I could not imagine, and it was frankly rundown, a dive, in fact. I did have to agree with his remarks about the holiday, however. We could see Swedish tourists outside fainting in the December heat wave.

There were palm trees festooned with holiday decorations visible through the dark blue windows. Jolly plastic Santas and reindeers melted in the heavy heat. Garlands drooped sadly. We were sitting as close as we dared to a dangerous fan that vainly tried to stir up the turgid air. My friend was talking, however, and this was good news for me. In fact, he seemed swept up in an odd wave of nostalgia on this searing winter afternoon that needed some cheer to it, given the imminence of the big day itself.

"You see," he said, tipping the battered fedora back on his old head, "I never, in the old days, had any visions of sugar-fairies and reindeers and guys named Frosty because all I knew was the seamy world of the police-blotter, the run-down underside of what we called life then. Back in those days, if I saw some socks dangling from a mantle, I'd start looking for the rest of the body. See what I mean? There were no smiling faces upturned in their big woolly mufflers asking me for a free turkey."

I told him that his days as a detective had certainly hardened him.

"Now, I'm as soft as taffy," he said, "but in those days, I was hard, all right. I was hard as the Big Rock Candy Mountain until one Christmas years ago."

I picked up my notebook and opened it and searched for my old fountain pen, the one I hoped wouldn't leak onto my shirt. We were drinking shots of Black Label in the late afternoon and smoking cigarettes for fun.

"You see," said the Old Detective, lighting up another one with his old brass lighter, "I took on a case one Christmas for a guy named Kringle, a peppy old guy with a white beard who beat the elevator up to my office one crisp December day when the new smog hung from the eves in frozen stillness and the crunch of snow could be heard on half the sound stages around town. Kringle was an enthusiastic bird, full of fizz, and he poured out a story as old as time itself. It was all the usual stuff: flying fantasies, chimneys, whips, something about a red nose and some implications about Sears that couldn't be proved. I'd been down that street before."

"What street?" I asked.

"In those days, Sears had a store over on Santa Monica Boulevard."

"You know what I mean."

"Do I? I'm feeling good today, I'm feeling frisky. Are you getting this down?"

I told him I was getting it down. Actually, I wasn't. The minute he had mentioned Kringle and Christmas in the same sentence, I had merely written the word "Xmas" on my notepad and was now idly tracing over and over the X. I began to try to draw snowmen.

"Now, on that day of cheer and good will—you getting this all down?—there was a Christmas party going on across the hall from my office. This was when I had magazines in nice magazine racks in the outside office and a great-looking secretary named Ruby who used to sit out there with her legs crossed."

I asked him if the correct word wasn't "gams".

"If I'd meant gams I'd have said gams. Ruby had legs a mile and a half long and a mother who couldn't remember her name, she was so far gone on hooch. That's hooch—h-double-o-c-h." I pretended to write something. Actually, I had drawn a reindeer on its back with its legs straight up and with two X's for eyes. But the Old Detective seemed satisfied and continued on.

"After a while—mostly because of Ruby—the party spilled over across the hall to my place. The usual bunch of crazies from the Five-Star/Hopeless Talent Agency were around. You remember the name Paul Bunyan?"

"The giant lumberjack?"

"Yeah. Well, he was there."

I asked him how that could be, since I remembered Paul Bunyan as being mythical at best and imaginary at worst.

"You're too young, you wouldn't remember," he replied, puffing smoke. "By that time in his career he was good for occasional guest shots on the Gary Moore Show and such. He was getting bookings, is what I mean. Miss Mysterioso—Mistress of Mystery? played the organ? —everybody remembers her. Well, she was there with some potato salad that was really good, as I recall, and she had on a green and red sequined number that showed the two or three things about her that were no mystery at all."

I said I understood him to mean that Miss Mysterioso—the Mistress of Mystery—was a looker.

"You got that right, son," he smiled. "Curves up ahead or whatever the road sign says, if you subscribe to my meaning."

I asked if perhaps she had great gams.

"If I'd meant she had gams, I'd have mentioned it," he said stiffly. "That Argentine guy who had the trained bears showed up with some fruit cake that had candied mushrooms in it and the girls from downstairs at Henrietta's House of Hair came upstairs and put on some Chet Baker records and started dancing with each other real slow. There was a big old traditional roast albatross with that sage and treacle dressing. After a while, even old Kringle had a few shots of toddy and pretty soon he was doing the stroll or whatever they called it in those days. At one point, even the bears were doing it. The party got pretty wild and I lost track of Kringle. You see, I had forgotten to tell Ruby to sweep my rod off the top of my desk."

I asked if it was common practice in those days for a detective to leave a loaded weapon out on the desk. Was this Kringle so intimidating?

"I wasn't intimidated by anything in those days," he said roughly. "But you never know. Remember, I was as hard as the Big Rock Candy mountains and thought Christmas was just a fancy way of spelling burglary. I was on alert, let me put it that way."

"Fine," I said and pretended to cross something out and write something in.

"Now, I was leaning in on Miss Mysterioso pretty good—and believe me, there was a lot to lean over—when we heard the shot."

"A gun shot?"

"That's what everyone figured."

"Kringle shot himself?"

"Did I say that? Of course, that's the first thing an amateur like you would think."

I suggested that he tell me, then, what actually happened.

"It was the crack of a tree splitting. It seems this Bunyan guy was outside chopping down a magnolia tree. He wanted a magnolia to give to Miss Mysterioso because he was so in love with her. Sometimes a guy like that will just go crazy over a woman."

I replied that, of course, I'd been down that street before.

"Nearly everyone in this town has been down Santa Monica Boulevard, sometimes twice a day. You ain't heard the half of it, kid," he snapped.

"The half I've heard isn't exactly worth writing down," I snapped back. He stared at me for a moment.

"Should I be getting royalties for these stories about me?" He looked serious.

"No," I lied. "Because I don't get any."

"Good," he said. "Royalty is a mistaken idea anyway, much like Christmas, or at least that's what Kringle found out."

I said he was certainly aware, wasn't he, that there had been a famous movie made about a man named Kringle who looks just like Santa Claus?

"This wasn't the same guy," he said. "This guy's name was Ferdinand Kringle. Ferdinand L. Kringle, I can see the name on the file folder to this day."

I told him he certainly had a good memory.

"No," he muttered, "I had the file out last night because I'm thinking of writing up some of my adventures myself, cut out the middle man, so to speak."

"You mean me?"

"Do I? You be the judge. You getting this down?"

I started to write. Yes, I said grimly, I'm getting this down.

"Good. There was a shot later on, by the way, so if you were on a computer, you could just save the word 'shot' onto a file somewhere and have it ready to reinsert when I get to the shot part."

I said thanks and when was he going to get to the shot part?

"When I'm good and ready," he snarled. "We better think about modernizing some. I think we ought to buy a computer and then you could get online and do some networking and maybe we could make some money off these stories about me."

I replied that I had every hope that in the future there might be some money from these stories and of course some of that money would be his and in the meantime, I might see my way clear to advancing him a little something.

"Ah," he said. "That's the Christmas spirit. Now we're talking. You write and I'll talk. I'm thinking of getting a hot tub, you know? I'll soak and reminisce and you'll get it all down on the mainframe. Now, Christmas was all humbug to me, remember? So, when the boys in blue found Kringle under the Hollywood Christmas Tree of Lights, strangled with those awful twisted green and red double wires they used to have and bearing strange marks on his body, they normally wouldn't have guessed that I was at all involved. Unfortunately, he had my card in his pocket."

I asked him if they thought he'd killed Kringle. He looked pensive and faraway for a moment.

"They were hoping I'd done something," he said. "I didn't have many friends down at Hollywood Division in those days. I'd embarrassed those boys one too many times. They hauled me down to headquarters in a black and white and set me up under that one bare light bulb they were so proud of and they all sat back in the shadows and started firing questions at me that I couldn't answer. Most of them seemed to be about a drunk reindeer and Sears. I didn't think much of it to do with Christmas, frankly."

I asked him if by any chance we were somehow talking about "Rudolph, the Red-nosed Reindeer," a Christmas ditty that was originally composed—as I understood it—by a man in Chicago who worked for Sears.

"No," he said. "There was no singing on this one. This turned out to be only about a drunk reindeer named Osborne who may or may not have had a red nose. It's immaterial whether it was red or not. Seems he'd been breaking into Sears on Santa Monica Boulevard and stealing power tools. Some of the marks on Kringle matched the dado head on a Craftsman Table Saw, lucky for me. After thirty-six hours of questioning, they had to let me go. When I got back to the office, the party was still going on. I managed to find Miss Mysterioso. Paul Bunyan had her backed up against a moonlit brick wall covered with ivy and was telling her a lot of lies. I said, 'Is this guy bothering you?' and she said '*You* bother me, big boy. This guy is just plain annoying' and so I told Bunyan to take a hike and he launched off into the same story he'd already told on the *Merv Griffin Show* about this hike he once took with a blue ox and I pretended to look interested—the same as Merv had— and after awhile he got so wrapped up in laughing at his own jokes that I just walked her away into the moonlight and the rest is history."

Where, I asked, is this history written?

"In the hearts of Mankind," the Old Detective answered, seriously enough. "You see, she was very good to me. It kind of changed my mind about Christmas, after all. She had a pair of gams on her that could melt the heart of Black Peter himself."

So there was some justice to the season after all, in those long-gone days. I like to think there was, anyway, back when Santa had a tan and Mrs. Santa was named Monica and wore a bikini and sunglasses and after the parade down Hollywood Boulevard they'd get together a bunch of their friends and they'd all pile into their big old turquoise convertible and bomb out to Palm Springs for Christmas because it was the kind of place where the Prince of Peace himself would feel right at home, out there among the roadrunners and the cactuses and the Joshua trees, with the stars out at night, so many you could never hope to imagine them all, and the natural evils of the human spirit damped down for once and calmed on this one night of all nights in our mysterious town.

The Hall of No Eye Contact

☼

We took kids the other night to the Fair in the pouring rain and all they wanted to do was eat and ride on rides and shovel money into the grasping hands of the carnies who man the gyp booths. And have fun. Cold, pouring down rain, seven to ten year-old kids; you get the picture. My grand-niece held my hand as we strode through the wall of neon foods. My twin grandnephews clutched their stash of posters and gyp trinkets as if gold, holding hands with Oona. Nick the neighbor kid rode the toughest rides and supervised us all, since seventh grade gives you a responsibility, it turns out, one deeper than I'd remembered. As for the world of gyp and fear, believe me, I'm up to date on the Octopus, the Whirl of Death and the Shoot-Something-That-Looks-Easy-But-Isn't in a futile attempt to win the giant SpongeBob doll. I've been there. I've had fun. But now is the second day and the true fair calls.

The Mystery calls. If you need me, I'll be somewhere in between Egg Artistry and the Swine Gate.

We got to the fair around three in the afternoon and the attendant populace seemed stunned in the sunlight and warmth, under the great mountain Tahoma in the Puyallup Valley. At four o'clock the teeners began to arrive in force and the Midway began to resound with the chilling shrieks that make the fair more than what it is. There is something comforting in this, I realized. The fair without the sex and screaming is not really a fair. It's just an exhibition.

We visit slabs of bees and cases of slugs devouring equally slimy boleti, slugs of the Northwest, mushrooms of the Northwest and reach finally the Grange displays, a whole hall of sloped agricultural layouts, each Grange responsible for filling five hundred or so square feet of space with neatly organized displays of their fruits and vegetables, their agricultural heritage fast disappearing under the mighty surge of suburban sprawl seeping out from Seattle and Tacoma. Our local Grange in Mystery Island is the Gig Harbor Grange, an old creaky building now bounded by a golf course and a traffic light, once a lonely outpost at the head of Wollochet creek, where salmon now need human protection to spawn. The grangers have bravely lined up carrots and plums and apples and found a theme to wrap it all around and at the top have placed mason jars of bright green and yellow and red jams and jellies so that lights shine through them in a beautiful display of something so touching I can barely look too long. I sit down on one of the log benches and scribble notes, avoiding the glances of huge fat white guys in black tank tops who are desperately trying to organize their kids into a move on the sluggish indoor pool where the Demonstration Chinook Salmon swim aimlessly over the copper bottom of tossed pennies. In the Old Days, copper was one of the most valuable things in the Old People world. Big beaten sheets of it were made into three-partitioned artworks of immense value and meaning lost to us now, like the teeth of beavers lost.

We eat fried clams and halibut and chips, we drink Doctor Pepper without fear, we have a corn dog and a scone, we ingest the curly fries, all on the way to the Halls of Hapless Animals, lined up in rows, caring little for us. There are rabbits of every description, birds so many that their cages form an avian weir to herd and trap humans. Game birds painted by opiumated Chinese. Bunnies and squabs and cavies and nice 4-H dogs lying peacefully on benches to be viewed, their owners sitting beside them ready to answer questions.

Percherons in beautiful stalls turn their gigantic butts to us, cows ignore us, goats eat in spite of us, llamas do not spit even at us, even once. We traipse to the Hall of Hair, also known as the Hall of No Eye Contact or the adjoining Hall of Sewing, Lounging and Pain Relief. Divorce is ripping our adult ranks, did I mention we were adults? Don't we have problems? Well, I guess we do. Last year's Barbie is this year's divorcee.

We are nearing the Hall of Modern Living and in fact we have entered the all too human area of the Great Fair. Healing creams and wellness crystals and lounge beds and massage pods and Saunas and hot tubs, TV knives, fair hair, stop smoking, heal, rest lounge. Hedonism seems to be the order of the day, care for the self. There seem to be no booths for Calvinism, for restraint, for punishment or discipline or pain.

Outside, the huge grandstand has filled with humans and Styx or something like it plays loud and the huge crowd of bell-bottomed and tattooed hedonists scream and lights flash. It is dark. Then it is very light. Kick drums boom, Munch-like screamers scream. It is dark. Then it is very light.

In the Hobby Horse Hall (the Hall of Tristram Shandy) comes a great moment, one in which the full power of the great Fair Mystery descends upon me like a Giant Neon Screaming Hammer of Shrieking Delight. It's a huge hall of compulsions, filled to the brim with people's need to collect Hello Kitty paraphernalia, the pressing need to fill a whole case with watches, or bees or stuffed penguins or polar bears or miniature automobiles, or—in the past—shoulder pads. That wonderful board of shoulder pads is gone now, but Garfield is alive and well, thousands of him crammed yellow into the case next to the Elvis memorabilia. There are the rocket guys, the telescope guys, the ham radio guys and most of all, those kings of Nerds, the Model Railroad Guys. Out in the middle of all these cases of dolls and guys, the N-Gauge railroad makes a big oblong loop. The little trains roll through the little scenery. As usual, I stand and stare too long. The Big Blonde is already over among the dollhouses.

The dollhouses are deep, as usual, but I'm about to turn back to the beloved trains when my eyes are whacked over their little eyeball heads by the Best of Show winner, a stunning three-quarters-of-an-inch-equals-one- foot model of an old country train station. The left half is as it was eighty years ago and its right as it is today, that is in complete and derelict disrepair. In the pristine left-hand half, a lonely miniature child sits crumpled on a bench, weeping and awaiting, presumably, some miniature human or other picking him up and taking him somewhere. On the right-hand side, the side of the modern world, an old man supported by a young couple points across the modeler's timeline divide and remembers something we cannot hear, probably because sound based on three-quarter inch to the foot ratios tagged to decibels and frequencies would be beyond quick.

A little card tells you only that on a disturbing model day eighty years ago, a lonely orphan took the train to his new home. Above are many telephone wires and bulbous crows. All it needs is music, but scaled music would be pitched very high (or low) and gone in a second. Or last forever. It all depends on where you start.

In other words, scaling is a deep subject. Things can be hidden in the spaces between scales, simply because there must be spaces between scales, otherwise there would be only one scale and this cannot be true. The grand-nephews and nieces' father is in jail, meth is suspected, murder is accused. The little ones cling to the Big Beautiful Blonde's hands in the rollicking fair night. The scales are of divorce, of murder, of accusations and fear, of little kids who need help, of the love that knows no reasoning, of fun, of this fair, of this summer, of this fall. The Big Blonde knows that these kids need to remember this awful year as the year they had a lot of fun at the fair, on one whacky night at least. A scale away, the adults are divorcing and arguing and posing and whining. She and I have fun no matter what scale we're in. We know where to look for fun. We have our picture taken in the black-and-white booth and, as every year, the woman who runs the booths remembers us. We laugh and chat. It's the fair. We should have jammed the kids in the booth the other night and had their picture. Next year we'll remember. Next year.

STATE FAIR BARBIE GOES TO THE FAIR

Elsie and I went to the big State Fair over in Beaverteeth and had the time of our lives. I particularly enjoyed the big jolly fistfight in the Swine Building right after

Elvis kissed Barbie. It was a miracle that Elvis won the race as well, seeing as how that bad guy who seems good—the one with the sweeping blonde hair—how that guy and his pals took advantage of Elve. I enjoyed the three musical numbers I had, singing and playing the standup bass behind Elvis, especially the one where I look goofy and the camera comes in and takes what is called a "close-up" of me. I'm the guy in the bandanna with the big buckteeth. Elsie says you can't miss me. I also enjoyed how Elvis won the race, but it was really best at the start when that bad girl with the black hair cut straight across her forehead waved her bra to start the race. I've seen a lot of pictures of her tied up and real naked in barns and other rustic environments and I've got to say, I enjoy looking at her just as much as I enjoy looking at Barbie, semi-clothed in her adorable State Fair Barbie outfit.

But there's more to the Fair than just singing and fighting and racing, and the thrilling competition for Elvis between good girls in sleeveless plaid shirts with the shirt-tails tied so as to show off their adorable tummies and bad girls, tied up with gags in their mouths and perched up on five inch heels and gripped in leather corsets, that's for sure. I've been going to the damn thing for many a year and I've had a lot of thoughts over those years and one of them is the one that sums up most of the others and that is the thought that thinks that a Fair, no matter how you look at it, comes down to pretty much one thing; and that thing is, in a word, exhibition.

This year, the exhibit of the giant pumpkins takes up maybe a quarter of the Hall of Agriculture and one of them weighs—get this—over eleven hundred pounds. The odd thing about it is that the great whitish, yellowish thing looks so subdued by its own immense weight that it seems to melt into the concrete floor. Its grower disqualified himself from the annual competition because he had discovered a tiny flaw, a hole so small that Judges might easily have overlooked and so awarded him the blue ribbon. He said that he'd won so many other years before that he'd decided to give his other competitors a chance or two. The new winners, in the nine hundred pound range, also looked collapsed under their own immense weights, their ribbons adding little to their gravitational demise.

And everybody and everything at the State Fair is an exhibit of one kind or another and I'll explain what I mean by first pointing out that the opposite of exhibition has got to be inhibition. Inhibition wouldn't make for much of a Fair. I suspect you'd see a lot of people with thick glasses in cardigan sweaters clutching books while milling uncertainly around the fairgrounds, each nervous about the other, muttering clever comments to themselves about how stupid everyone else is and pointedly not going to see the giant pumpkins. The Inhibition Fair wouldn't be much fun, whereas at the Fair of Exhibition, as I'm sure I point out every year, particularly the night time can seem to be a sexual ritual of some kind. Particularly out among the Whirling Ding

Dongs of Death, there is a parade of the voluptuous bodies of teenage girls with virtually no clothes on, topped with cowboy hats, or garish pirate or cowboy hats or other souvenir headgear. Their boyfriends—shaved heads, multiple earrings, dressed inevitably in baggy black—clutch feverishly at them, steering them toward night and neon light and screaming fun. This year they've all bought the skintight bellbottom jeans cut so low that they, much like the Giant Pumpkins, seem drawn toward the earth with some huge sexual finality. Their outthrust naked stomachs, their breasts exposed in Target tops, the sleeves gathered high on their little shoulders to bare more flesh. The day is warm and school is finished for one more monumental day. Pregnancy lies only dimly ahead. The sun is going down into the Magritte-green sky and the twisting neon lights of Fear and Death hoist themselves up into the coming darkness. The night is young.

Unlike Elvis and Barbie, they don't race, they don't fight, they don't sing. But they're not unaware of the fact that they are, as well, on exhibit.

One of the best things about the Fair is: The Hall of Modern Living, or, as I call it, the Hall of No Eye Contact. Here's how modern it is; about a third of the exhibitors wear microphones and they demonstrate, they slice and they dice and so the experience is slightly what we call out at my place surreal. For instance, there are two girls, the Vita-health girl and the Mop girl, no one in front of them, talking to each other quietly although they are thirty feet apart. They have on microphones. They are wired. It's the Hall of Modern Living. Don't talk to me about modern. I've been there. The John Birch Society is set up next to the Gutter demonstration, where water flows down a roof and into a gutter and magically, no branches or moss even goes into the gutter. If you make eye contact with any of these people, you are doomed. They've got you. You have to be strong to look away, to not answer, to keep moving, to not respond. The Hall of No Eye Contact is Exhibitors Gone Wild, no holds barred, nothing restrained. You are the hunted.

Barbie bought the State Fair Hair at the fair this year. It's a hell of a kind of pony tail but it sticks way up high and it exactly matches the original hair that Barbie went to the fair with. She also bought the dachshund purse, the one that not only looks like a dachshund but is the same exact size. State Fair Barbie, comes with adorable dachshund purse. Pilot Jeff sold separately. One of the best things about the Fair is: The midway, the neon, the shrieking and wailing of the doomed customers, the grinding of oily old machines held together by the presumably limited skill and interest of people who might be able to make more money back brewing meth in severely depressed rural areas were it not for the needs of exhibition. You're going to want to see the cases of preserves, the hall of grange artwork, the huge geometric arrangements of fruits and vegetables, the giant pumpkins, sagging under their own immense orange weights. The crossbows, the fish receiving coins, the Army Corps of Engineers (the Army Corps of Dioramas), the flood plain demo diorama, every year. We ate fried oysters and french-fries at the seafood stand. You know you've got good food coming when you notice that most of the customers are Nisqually or Puyallup people. The corn dogs were good this year, the scones excellent and the burgers large and smothered with Walla-Walla onions. The hall of quilts and sewing, the many artworks and paintings and sculptures included a couple of the finest Art of The Insane pictures I've ever seen, just like that guy Flamnigan on TV.

It's the Fair, in other words. Get there or be square. They're trying to tell me that Elvis is dead, but he isn't, not when you can go to the Fair. Look out for Barbie, but the best thing is that every year, when the huge clouds turn orange overhead and the lights of the Insane Rides pop out and the darkness descends and the shrieking idiots are flung upward hundreds of feet in the air and the big moon rises, Elsie and I go to the lineup of photo booths and we wait with all the teenage bad girls—the girls who have rings in places you don't want to know about, whose heads are shaved in ways unthought by normalcy, whose hair is colored as if by the midway itself—and we squeeze the two of us into the booth and draw the curtain and insert the dollar bills and have four black and white pictures taken of ourselves. We wait outside, joking with the bad girls and after a while the strip of photos comes out and there we are, the two of us.

I should mention the deep things, too. There's the huge model of the volcano that towers over the fairgrounds, showing what will happen to us if it blows, when it blows. And there is the always unspoken, the end of summer near, the eating of the corn, the drying of the stalks, the pumpkin vine dies away and leaves the orange thing. The leaves begin to blow, the maples' edges look dark red and then, too quickly, yellow. Death is upon us. And so we find ourselves back at the Fair of Inhibition, the Fair of No Location (the Fair of No State, stateless in fact, a thing unexpressed, a thing of no qualities). Another year. Another fair. Four more black and white pictures. Elsie looks cute as can be and I look older, but okay, I guess.

And you know, next year I'm not even going to the fistfight. I want to spend more time with the rabbits and pigeons. That's where the action is. Enough striving, enough competition. Exhibition, that's what it's all about. Did you see the size of the feathers on that pigeon's feet? Wow. Blue ribbon, red ribbon, green ribbon. Who cares? Not me. We closed the place down. We drove home below half a moon, as if the Chainsaw Sculptor of the Night had neatly cut it down the middle. It was only half the fair, the adult half. I looked back on the kid half with more pleasure than I'd thought, back there in the other scale, in the pouring down rain. We drive home to Mystery Island over the many bridges and half a moon shines over the water and summer is not quite gone.

Elmer

The Tower of All Locations

✿

One day in Fresno—a modest enough city set in the great flat middle of California—young Mrs. Garabendian went outside and realized there was no good reason why she should ever go inside again. From that time on, as far as we knew, she never entered a building of any kind. At first we thought that Mrs. Garabendian was a kind of camper, an entirely logical thought because her outdoorness happened in the nineteen-fifties of the Last Century, long before the word "homeless" came to be applied to people who simply didn't or couldn't or wouldn't live in buildings. But she was not a camper. She was never seen in less than high heels, for instance. She never, so she said, built a fire or whittled a stick.

Mrs. Garabendian was not an old woman. On that one day, she was what was then called a young matron and in that long-gone time she might be not incorrectly thought to have been wearing a smart sleeveless summer dress, vertically striped, perhaps, with a strand of pearls encircling her young throat; her hair might have been paged and blonde, she might have been holding a large transparent plastic salad spoon, she might have had on an apron; she might have been standing beside a marvelous Household Invention, one making her housework easier, allowing her, presumably, to wear the smart sleeveless dress and the pearls and high heels at home during the day and produce as well attractive food for a grateful family who did not smoke cigarettes, although she occasionally did—outside—while her husband, Mr. Garabendian, smoked his pipe inside.

This vision of Mrs. Garabendian would have fit pretty much exactly into the visions of Mr. Garabendian, the pipe smoker. These visions he produced on large sheets of thick white paper at his drawing board down at the advertising agency on Muscat Street where he worked day after ceaseless day in Fresno, in the great flat middle of the State of California.

On the morning Mrs. Garabendian walked outside, never to return inside, she was, in fact, wearing a dress quite like the one mentioned and, indeed, there was about her throat a strand of cultured pearls and while she was not carrying a spoon, she did have a Bakelite salad-fork salad-serving implement—half of which was a large spoon, the other half a large fork—nestled in the big pocket of her apron. The apron itself was embroidered with cocktail glasses spouting bubbles and had a gathered trim of lime-colored gauze. As she stood outside and looked back into her ex-house she saw clearly, through the screen door, her ex-kitchen. In it was set a table with a chartreuse green tablecloth topped by a gelatinized roast of lamb garnished with sprigs of rosemary, the whole finished with candied leaves of mint. She noticed that glasses of tall blue liquid were ranged alongside this dish, glasses full of a blue gelatinous something she also could not quite identify. Where had it all come from? Certainly not from her.

This was a problem, she thought. That she could not remember.

Mrs. Garabendian, young matron, stood outside then and shivered and gazed up into the sky above, second-guessing her failing memory. She shivered in spite of it being a hot summer day, one quite normal for Fresno, out in the great flat middle of the State of California.

The sun had yet to set. The evening was a ways off and with it the return of Mr. Garabendian from his job, about which she knew very little. Mr. Garabendian drove a car, this she knew, and had a first name, although she thought she might have forgotten it as well. The sun beat down upon her, belying her coldness. There were little weeds crushed by her high heels in the back yard. She had once made them into a kind of scissors when she was a kid on Ash Street, in Fresno, in the great flat middle of the State of California, but she was too old now, on the day she went outside, never to go inside again, ever.

After awhile she sat down on the red swing that was one of her children's and she lit a cigarette—a Tareyton, a pack of which she'd carried in the other pocket of her apron—and crossed her legs and slender feet in high heels, keeping one spike dug into the childish sand. Inside her ex-house, the clunky old-fashioned phone had begun to ring. It rang and rang and then stopped. Mr. Garabendian drove up and after awhile looked for her and a discussion ensued. She did not go inside.

Mr. Garabendian eventually coped with the situation and in fact, came to somewhat like doing the housework and the cooking inside. He found so many flaws in the traditional procedures (the which he ascertained in the first year of her outdoorness by angrily shouting questions out the back screen door to Mrs. Garabendian) that he was driven into a remaining-lifelong fit of invention in which he was to find entirely new and interesting ways to clean and dust and polish and produce attractive, even gelatinized, meals. He eventually profited greatly at all these activities, quite proudly. Before this, Mr. Garabendian had been merely employed in the execution of drawings of smart modern housewives in sleeveless dresses preparing meals with relative ease because of the purchase of one household appliance or another, somewhere in Fresno. He eventually forgot even the name of the street where his old advertising agency sat. He worked out of the house. He made a fortune.

Once she began to live outside, Mrs. Garabendian did not care in the least, ever again, about Mr. Garabendian. Remarkably, she kept up a normal life, at least by her own standards, which admittedly were not entirely commonplace. She went places. It was late in the nineteen-fifties and the Garabendians had two cars. Her car was the older of the two, a 1952 Chevrolet convertible that had once seemed to set her and Mr. Garabendian apart from others on Olive Street. When she drove to her various destinations, she would not go inside any building. At a bridge party, for instance, she would sit just outside the front door, rain or shine, dressed correctly, legs crossed at the ankles, just above her high-heeled feet, and she would play her bridge hands through the screen door. She did not like it inside, she would explain, somewhat vaguely. Since none of her friends knew her very well, but liked her very much, she was indulged more than you might expect. She had one hell of a personality, everyone said.

She would never put the top up on the car and when Mr. Garabendian appropriated the garage in order to build prototypes of his inventions, he found that the actual cloth top to her car had in fact rotted away. This made him furious, but this did not bother in the least Mrs. Garabendian, who by that time was living up in—or down in, depending on how you looked at it—the Tower of All Locations.

The Tower of All Locations, Mrs. Garabendian would explain (had anyone asked), was not a building. Per se. It was a tower and it did not have an inside in which to live. It had no exact location, in fact. It was merely her address. Her children, as they grew, attested to the fact that they had never been there, nor did they know where the Tower of All Locations was, although they knew its address.

Mrs. Garabendian had many loyal friends, all of them women much like herself. Mrs. Mikelian and Mrs. Avenasian were particularly sure to get Mrs. Garabendian plates of food or drinks at parties, she outside, in rain or fog or heat.

Mr. Garabendian eventually tired of asking her questions and merely left (hot) TV dinners outside for her on the seat of the swing. Mr. Garabendian had, at this time, invented TV dinners. He had also invented something he'd been working on for quite a long time, his Imaginary Other Family.

When Mrs. Garabendian went to the nursery, she wore heels and sleeveless dresses, except on those cold winter days when the tule fog pressed down upon Fresno and then she might wear a cashmere sweater thrown over her bare shoulders and of course a string of pearls around her neck. In summer weather, when the temperature could easily top one hundred degrees, she might wear sleeveless blouses with collars up and down below, tight black toreador pants and high heels. These clothes, and her considerable underwear, she would wash at the Avenasian Laundromat on Palm Avenue with the help of her friend Mrs.

(Millie) Avenasian, who carefully inserted coins into the machines while Mrs. Garabendian paced the little parking area out in front, smoking Tareytons (later Marlboros) so as to avoid going inside anywhere. The years passed. The idea came to her of the Tower of all Locations at the laundromat.

Mrs. Garabendian took quite an interest in her back yard almost from the very first year that she went outside, never to go inside again. She had always been something of a gardener. She'd planted tomatoes and gourds and beans in the past. After awhile, she began to plant taller and more hardy things, starting only with the money she had in the pocket of the apron she wore on the day she walked outside. It turned out that Fresno was a place in which you could grow virtually anything.

She would drive down to the nursery, which was luckily only three Fresno-sized blocks away. Mr. Haggard, who owned the nursery, would be glad to see her. At first, he sold her several small plants, and answered her questions about propagation and root layering. He suggested to her that she might buy more plants.

"Au contraire, babe," said Mrs. Garabendian. (This was the way she talked and you just got used to it.) She bought instead a small bottle of rooting hormone. At first, Mrs. Garabendian planted the back yard and then she organized her plantings into a kind of walkway and then finally into a maze of sorts. It was a pretty good-sized backyard, these being the days in Fresno when backyards were important to people. Whether she had laid a pattern out before she planted or whether she made one up as she went along, we never knew. After awhile, you couldn't see her in there anymore, no matter how hard you peered through the fence or over the fence or under the fence.

She decided to take responsibility for exactly what already existed in her life. To achieve this, in order to see what exactly was in her life, with complete honesty, she decided she would need a vantage point. The best vantage point she could think of, in the great flatness of the San Joaquin Valley, was a tower, there being no natural features of any great height anywhere near, unless you counted the stunning height of the Sierra Nevada mountains to the east which were so far away and so vast that she did not—in fact—count them.

Taking responsibility for her actual life, as it actually existed, meant not giving any meaning to her life beyond the fact that everything in it was her direct responsibility. The mountains were not in her life and were therefore not her responsibility. Height was her problem, height and vision.

As we found out later, she dug down. She dug a maze into the ground, a network of tunnels and caves that led nowhere, or so it seemed. In fact, it led to the Tower of All Locations, but Mrs. Garabendian would never tell anyone that. Only she knew.

One of the complaints that Mrs. Garabendian felt toward Mr. Garabendian, was that of a feeling of being smothered alive. She felt that not only could she not breathe in his presence, but that as well, she could not see. If she could not see, if she could not breathe, she could not ascertain her exact responsibility. She did not know if she was acted upon or if she acted alone. When she was serious about seeing, she always thought of the Municipal Water Tower of Fresno and how, from its Renaissance-like, scenic balcony, one could probably see a long distance, if by some miracle one were allowed up there. When the one allowed could see a long distance, then that one could locate objects, things, thoughts, people, friends, friends' dogs, stores, and so forth. One took responsibility for the view. A view was a life. A life with a view was a life of full responsibility. To this, Mrs. Garabendian aspired. She had a vision, in other words.

So Mrs. Garabendian took as her model the Fresno Municipal Water Tower, a San Joaquin Valley symbol of township and aridity. She had seen the water tower for her entire life in Fresno. It was a kind of Renaissance Italian tower, round and yet squat, with a red tile roof and columns and arches beneath, built in this elegant style probably to disguise its utilitarian nature, which was to store as much water as possible in a place, the San Joaquin Valley, and in particular the City of Fresno, that saw little enough rainfall each year. Although the mass of clouds from off the Pacific ocean lifted to rise over the Sierra Nevadas to Fresno's east and dropped their moisture up there, the water flowed down the west side of the huge mountain range in great rushes, making flooding spring rivers, the Kern and the Kings and the San Joaquin. The water came through but it came through fast and deep and before the baking summers were over, the rivers were nearly dry. Mrs. Garabendian cared not. Her water came out of the hose tap in the back yard and she bought hoses and later plastic pipe in order to channel it into the irrigation system she set up. Later, it was said, she dug deep enough to unearth a spring or two and so provide water for a myriad of structures she built to surround and protect the Tower of All Locations.

The town of Fresno at that time had a lot of people in it, people who mostly served in one way or another the great surrounding crops of grapes and raisins and apricots and cotton. These people all needed water—even people from Oklahoma who lived in small houses they did not own—and the ranchers needed the people and if you needed people they would thirst and someone had to store water so that they might drink twice or thrice a day, and deeply, in order that they might properly harvest or account or ship the grapes or fertilize the grapes or crop-dust the grapes or market the grapes or advertise the grapes or make up pictures of smartly-dressed housewives in sleeveless dresses with strings of pearls and high heels using grapes in some form or another in an attractive modern kitchen, made even more modern by the addition of clever household appliances and a few lines of peppy type that meant something to someone, in the pages of *Look* or *Life* or even the local *Fresno Bee* newspaper, which we delivered.

Since Mrs. Garabendian felt she could not see properly, she therefore decided to build a tower. But she did not want it to be seen. To hide it, she built instead a maze. The tower was set in the maze, but it was in fact under it, was underground. It was an upside-down tower. There was a thing in Fresno already called the Underground Gardens. She had never been there either, as she had never been up in the Fresno Water Tower, but she understood, from reading a brochure that Minnie Minasian procured for her, that the Underground Gardens were the creation of a man who carved out rooms under the tough ground of Fresno, in the great flat middle of the State of California. Mrs. Garabendian's maze avenues were planted oleanders, for the most part, a tough and poisonous plant of immense flowering ability that was at that time in favor as a highway divider out on Highway 99, the highway that one might use to escape from Fresno, if one so desired.

However, this was Mrs. Garabendian's thought; that a tower can see all the locations that it can see, the number depending only on its height. You can make a tower wider, but that gets you basically nowhere. It just allows more people onto the tower, but it doesn't increase their view. A Tower of All Locations is something that can be seen from *all* locations, so that it is, in fact, everywhere at once.

Is a tower a building? You are on it, not in it. If a tower is underground, what does it see? A tower is meant to see and to be seen. An underground tower is not seen; so what does it see?

As for us, we delivered the newspapers, me and my friends, in our little corner of Fresno, which was also Mrs. Garabendian's corner of Fresno. We folded the *Fresno Bee* into things that might sail and spin and we stuffed them neatly into the big canvas baskets draped over our rear fenders. We rode our fat-tired bicycles with one gear like demons, burning rubber marks into the backs of each others' canvas bags and then we would separate into groups of twos and threes and then we would be each alone, each on his solitary route, and there we would sail our *Fresno Bee* newspapers with our best accuracy onto the porches and occasionally roofs of the rows and rows of one-story houses, every seventh one of which had its double looking across the street from it, two down, and so forth and so on. It was a *system*, these interlaced houses and their repeated designs. The system needed news, evidently, and so we provided it because this was in the days before television was capable of providing much more than puppets and comics and floozies on a regular, black-and-white basis. The *Fresno Bee* was the news in those days, and those days are long gone.

In those days, a makeshift shelter of cardboard or wooden boxes or blankets was never deemed a building, and so it seemed to us that the true definition of a building was not whether it had been built or not, but whether it had been in fact addressed, numbered, that is, whether it had been exactly located, and whether it was, in fact, inside. Something that was inside was usually addressed and numbered and, by contrast, things that were outside were not. Parks, for instance, did not seem to have addresses, at least we didn't think so, nor did monuments or fishponds or fig orchards, all things indisputably of the outside. We never delivered the *Fresno Bee* to these places, and so we assumed they were Places Without Addresses.

Since Mrs. Garabendian liked to keep up with the news, and didn't want to share the *Fresno Bee* with Mr. Garabendian, she needed, she told me, a separate subscription and I answered that to ensure delivery and to satisfy the Powers That Be, that I'd need an address to deliver to and she stopped and looked down at me and said she'd have to think about it. Couldn't I just toss the paper over the fence? Then I'd have to note that the address was the usual Garabendian address and she stopped me and told me that she'd have to think about that. Every paper route has a couple of extra papers at the end of the day and since I lived next door to the Garabendians, I just tossed one of the extras over the fence, or—in later years—the towering hedges she'd planted.

It took years for Mrs. Garabendian to build a tower in a maze and then one day, as far as we knew, she climbed up it—or down into it— and never emerged from out of it or her maze again. That's all we know, to this day, and few of us are exactly sure what day that is.

None of us would follow Mrs. Garabendian and some of us still live in the neighborhood. Someone else delivers the newspapers in the afternoons and mornings these days and we have grown old and the Garabendian place still sits out on Olive Street although Mr. Garabendian died some years ago. Mrs. Garabendian is another matter.

Some say she still lives.

School Lunch Menus

✿

<u>PLAIN ELEMENTARY SCHOOL</u>

MON: Paper stack; Boneless Burrito; Paste; Kitten
   on a Stick; Milk-a-roni
TUES: White Bread on Toast; Glass of Sugar; See-
   through Lettuce; Liquid Milk
WED: Cake Sponge; Sugar Sandwich; Butter Plate;
   Cloth Pudding; Milk
THU: Simple Pie; Banana Splat; Sugar Mound;
   Blanched Cookie; Whey
FRI: Diaper Surprise; Clear Peaches; Steamed Cereal
   Boxes; Sugar; Milk

MYSTERY ISLAND SCHOOL FOR GIRLS

MON: Soft Eggs on a Mirror; Hard-Boiled Hollow
  Birds; Handful of Tacos; Milk
TUES: Rack of Clever Hans; Whisked Apple Fly; Coro-
  nation Ham; Nylon Bunnies; Big Carton
WED: Mystery Potato; Curd; Slippery Tart; Milk Pie;
  Leg Salad Sandwich; Clear Liquid
THU: Oysters Frightened By Chickens; Liver Mounds;
  Nest of Interesting Spiders; Mai Tai; Pack of
  Camels
FRI: Breast of Clam a la "Eddie;" Wieners in a Bas-
  ket Under a Blanket; Teacher's Surprise; Milk

EARNEST BOYS ACADEMY

MON: Beef throats; Smashed Leg; Hind Quarter; Gros
  Livers; Old-Fashioned Milk; Cigars
TUES: Flat Motor Pies; Fisherman's Regret; Loin of
  Fat; Stunned Ducks in Alcohol Sauce; Milk
WED: Tart Bottoms; Slick Fritters; Breasts of
  Toast; Sweetbreads in Hand; Cuckoo Punch; Cigars;
  Milk
THU: Roast Puffins; Revenge Pudding; Pancakes in
  Water; Baked Salad; Ring of Fire; Milk
FRI: Ducklings ala Moron; Smothered Rodents; Clos-
  et Pie; Turbo Skeletons; Champagne; Brandies;
  Cigars; Milk

WILLY LOMAN PUBLIC HIGH SCHOOL

MON: Horse Butter Sandwiches; Hot Jello Salad;
  French Kisses; Curb Cake; Milk
TUES: Toads in a Blanket in a Hole; Complicated
  Salad; Ice Bread; Lomax Pie; Milk Cocktail

WED: Hat With Cheese; Insurance Salad; V6 Bread;
   Field Surprise; Milk
THU: Battered Vegetables; Wax Wrappers; Wallet and
   Raisin Salad; Adult Milkshake
FRI: Fried Chuck; Paper Salad; Responsibility Pie;
   White Dessert; Retirement Milk

ALTERNATE CURRENT SCHOOL

MON: Eco-Veggie Bar; Rainbow Krazy Krunch; Twig
   Sticks; Turkey Straws; Cow Milk
TUES: Helpless Nuggets with Sour Sauce; Gator Tots;
   Trial Mix; White Milk
WED: False Rabbit Wedges; Farm Dip; Sloppy Jones;
   Birthday Cake; Goat Milk
THU: Meatless Hot Creatures; Sweetened Cherries;
   Meltdown on a Bun; Squares; Mother's Milk
FRI: Refried Fries; Early Dismissal Cup; Hemp
   Wheels; Party on a Bun; Dip; Sheep Milk

A Plea for Canine Acceptance

✿

As Canine Award shows steadily flood the cable channels, you may have noticed that many popular breeds of dog are never officially recognized. These excited television programs feature the same panoply of carefully groomed animals dragging around oddly dressed humans of varying sizes on lengths of string as, over and over, the same old favorites—Labrador, Cocker, Pekinese, Shepherd (German and otherwise) —are awarded the prestigious trophies, as if they alone were the only worthy recipients of the public's televised affection. (A side note: if this is a sport, then why can't the human handlers wear at least warm-up suits and running shoes for a properly athletic look? Why dress like Rotary members and School Board Supervisors? But, to my point...)

I'd like to suggest that it would be wise to take a look at some dogs that innovative breeders and handlers are promoting these days and, indeed, some that the public finds increasingly attractive. Please consider several newish breeds that I think deserve not only recognition and attention, but above all, love from people for whom dogs are something more than mere award-winners. These are valued family members with skills more directly tied to modern times than those outmoded skills celebrated by herding, sporting, toying, working and terriering. The AKC may not find them worthy, but I think you will.

Nova Scotia Cellphone Minute-Counting Retriever

A thoroughly modern breed of companion dog, this slim animal can keep track of minutes, make calculations up to nine places, remember calendar events and store an extensive list of phone contacts. The Nova Scotia is friendly, flat and colorful. The breed's ability to take pictures without being seen has been found useful by the Insurance Industry. The Nova particularly enjoys running with children, especially on weekends and after five o'clock. It may charge an extra amount for an early termination of its plan.

Breed Origins: Bred from the larger Flip Hounds and crossed with Hungarian Text-Messaging Herders, the Nova can be taken anywhere, though there is growing resistance to its presence at Broadway Shows and intimate restaurants.

Day-Old Danish Pointer

Also known as the Rack Dog in its native Denmark, this marked-down favorite of the urban young is a rare favorite. Two colors, cheese and prune, give the breed a distinctive look. It can be trained to track wounded game and can be found, tightly packaged, even in places like Utah roadside mini-marts, but it most readily adapts to urban environments and has indeed been specially bred for them in Europe. A strong taste for sugar makes it unacceptable as an all-season outdoor dog, but indoors it becomes an excellent coffee companion. This is a thick-boned, hearty breed of modest habits. The dog enjoys the Sunday *New York Times* and can even make hopeful phone calls to attractive young women.

Breed origins: Descended from the Black Pastry Hound of Central Europe, these dogs historically pointed at things in Vienna, particularly Puff Poodles.

Liberal Kansas Gun Dog

For the several hundred years in which black wild-eyed howling gun dogs were active members of the Wild Hunt—ducking and retrieving, bullets flying overhead—it was presumed they were willing and able participants in that ancient Germanic ritual. But early gunpowder firearms were remarkably inaccurate, spewing fire and shot in all directions and the traditional use of alcohol in the ritual continued unabated with the passing of years. Rumors swirled through the canine community in the 1700s that the number of loyal animals actually shot by drunken hunters was increasing at a rapid rate. In America, by the late 1900s, several strains of gundog began to exhibit traits that would eventually lead to the crossing of the Duck-Grabbing Retriever with the Cimarron Pointer by a breeder in Western Kansas to create the Kansas Liberal. This is an extremely unusual gun dog, naturally adept at taking guns away from hunters. The NRA has declared it to be an even greater threat than weeping inner-city mothers. The Liberal has been known to physically force inebriated hunters into twelve-step programs. It particularly enjoys digging shotgun-sized holes for the burial of weapons.

Breed origins: Of an ancient lineage, the friendly Liberal may be ultimately descended from primitive Gimme Dogs in Wales and northeast Germany.

Béarnaise Mountain Sauce Dog

The handsome Béarnaise will guard ½ cup white wine vinegar and was historically used to draw carts filled with 5 shallots, minced and at least 2 T. fresh tarragon. It is an excellent herding dog, particularly with

½ tsp. white pepper, but is equally willing to gather 4 egg yolks, ½ cup of boiling water and even 1 cup of warm clarified butter. It uses its size and strength to beat constantly with a wire whisk. Keeping the butter at the same temperature as the egg mixture can modify a tendency toward unprovoked aggression.

Breed Origins: An altogether ancient breed, it is said to be descended from the complex Hollandaise Dog.

Britney Mousketeer Spaniel

This most popular breed enjoys worldwide renown, not the least of which comes from its distinctive semi-nudity combined with the charm of a relatively empty head. The dog excels in mindless whispering while performing cheerleading lap dances. It inhabits huge stadiums and Internet dreams, where it can be readily Googled. It should not drive an automobile. The standard is for the dog to be heavy-set, notwithstanding its tendency toward bulimic behavior. Easily bred, waterproof and steadfast, it will endure pointless marriages of very short duration.

Breed origins: The Britney almost died out in the early years of this century, but was reconstituted in larger form by determined American Breeders. These dogs were originally used to haul in the floating nets of Armenian fisherman on the Elephantine Coast.

Mexican Zoot Hound

Extremely cool, this low-riding favorite is especially popular in the American Southwest, where it adapts easily to both desert temperatures and aesthetics. The draped coat of the long-haired variety sheds insults with aplomb. It is not easy to handle, however, and sports a strong independent streak. Young individuals favor late-model automobiles equipped with hydraulic lifts and cryptic phrases engraved in windows but in older animals, an image of the Virgin of Guadalupe often appears in the coat, which is long and literally drags on the ground. Crossed with the Pendleton Terrier in California in the 1950s and with the addition of Pachuco Mastiff stock from the Castro Valley, this breed naturally favors the music of Los Lobos.

Breed origins: In the smoky confines of Los Angeles nightclubs, this dog was originally bred to fight Caucasian-American servicemen of the Second World War. This practice has long since been discontinued.

Iditarod Refugee Dog

This active spitz-type dog, described by Jack London in *The Abysmal Race* (1919), is strong and athletic and will happily battle anyone in its pack at the flimsiest excuse. Still, this furtive charmer is frightened of sleds and will try to go south given any small opportunity. Shy and timid, it especially distrusts TV crews and has bad dreams about lonely athletic women who love dogs to the exclusion of everything else. One interesting trait is that of refusing to be numbered. The breed has been known to demand lucrative television contracts. At its worst, it simply runs away.

Breed Origins: This large dog originated in motels along highways leaving Alaska. It was originally bred for hauling loads of bulk gold bullion in impossible weather at high speed with only minimal amounts of dog food available.

Insatiable American Food Hound

Now said to be the most common of all American dogs, the Insatiable is quickly gaining acceptance worldwide, thanks to the rapid proliferation of delicious dog food to all corners of the globe. This breed, more than any other, recognizes the urgent need for dog food and demands it upon every occasion. These animals can purchase airline tickets, rent cars and open cans, especially the pull-tab variety, in their quest for more and more dog food. Certainly stalking is the ancient origin for this behavior, but the viewing of television food commercials—something this dog will do for hours—has largely taken the place of lynx, bear and vermin hunting.

Breed origins: At one time, nearly every small town had at least one of these dogs. When each had two, and their sexes were not the same, expansion of the breed was inevitable.

The Imaginary Dog Awards

✿

You won't find the Imaginary Dog Awards among your television list-ings. You won't find them in the plethora of awards shows that grace every channel, celebrating the sensibilities of shallowness like salt in the cracks of an evaporated pond. (Do I sound bitter?) The Imaginary Dog Awards are a fiction created by my dogs, or so I've come to believe. I'd include myself as a co-creator if I hadn't realized their uncanny canine power over me. My dogs have saved me from bitterness and in return, they've acquired a guy who can open a can of dog food with the best of them.

I do know a little something about real awards shows. For the last for-ty years or so, I've been one of the four members of a reputedly avant-garde comedy group called The Firesign Theatre and we've made a whole lot of audio records and CDs and a few video and film projects and done stage shows as well and in the process we've been nominated three times for a Grammy Award for Best Comedy Album. And we've lost each and every time. It's pathetic. We've rented limos and been to cocktail parties (even been on TV one memorable year that Jerry Seinfeld was nominated with us and so the powers-that-be thought it worthwhile to put our award on the tube), but each time we've lost. We've lost to Weird Al. We've lost to Carl Reiner and Mel Brooks and George Carlin. Lost like goats.

I've driven that lonely limo called "Just-Glad-to-be-Nominated," and believe me, the little shards of my stillborn acceptance speeches still rattle around my pitiful brain. It's positively embarrassing. I'd love to have risen from my seat, a fist punching the air as the TV cameras rolled, loved to have kissed the Blonde Bombshell and trotted up on stage with my partners to babble and be cut short by an orchestra eager to get home to its family, but it didn't happen and—because of dogs— I'm not bitter...or so it turns out. The Bombshell (her actual name is Oona) and I have adjusted to the inevitable. If we are not to be award-winners, we can at the very least become award-givers. And the awards we give out are called the Imaginary Dog Awards. Our life is all about dogs, after all. And our imaginations. And the dogs' eerie control over our imaginations. Let me explain.

I've heard it's been said by responsible scientific minds that dogs just might be entirely responsible for human civilization, that our complex web of social life would have been impossible were it not for the domestication of wolves, that without wolves raising the alarm and protecting humans and helping them hunt, humans wouldn't have had the time to construct civilization. This is a perfectly plausible theory, but large-scale and long-time, like Evolution. My theory is short-term, but weirdly logical, perhaps even stupid.

I have come to believe (I hope I'm not imagining this) that they are somehow able to control human imagination in order to get humans to give them more dog food. (My dogs, it turns out, love dog food more than anything in life and I'll bet yours aren't far behind.) The fact that I make up stories about them, ascribe to them human-like characteristics, have names for them, constantly talk to them, write about them... it's all their doing; they're controlling me, not the other way around. Ostensibly, it's human imagination at work, but suspiciously, it creates a fantasy that results in dogs getting more dog food, at least in the case of our awards.

Whatever their origin, the Imaginary Dog Awards are fun. Oona and I have been campers for all our life together and years ago we thought we'd cleverly instituted a family tradition; on the last night of any camping trip, we'd have an awards ceremony and award our many dogs some awards. We've had usually five or six dogs at a time for some thirty-five years, so you can imagine the amount of awards, given that we can usually manage two or three major camping trips a year, most often in the Eastern Sierras or the Sonoran Desert of Arizona or, more lately, in the Pacific Northwest, particularly on the beaches thereof. And we assumed that we were in charge.

At this point, your intelligence begins to kick in. Face the facts, Your Intelligence says, even though dogs don't actually care about the Dog Awards, don't even understand that you give them names, only care about dog food, other dogs and sleep, in that order; still, you and Oona are people who enjoy talking to your dogs and about them as if they're both human and understanding. You're right, I say, it's really just us two humans entertaining each other, of course, but the more we do it, the more the whole fabric of our imaginary dog conversations take on the spooky feel of reality. Ignoring the obvious is a big part of dog ownership, to be sure. Your Intelligence then points out that since dogs have a unique ability to make humans feel better about anything and everything, why not give them awards, for this if nothing else? Well, yeah, I say, and Your Intelligence quickly and politely mentions that Oona and I could easily have thought up the awards all by ourselves.

Well, we're certainly a big part of things. Indeed, if you watch enough TV, you'll notice that many shows feature a certain amount of carousing and we do try to fit right in. No matter where we are, no matter how unshaven (me)—how peaceful (her)—how uneager to return to what passes for Life, we humans manage to squirrel a bottle of champagne to crack open around the campfire on the last night in camp and drink out of those big plastic container-cups with covered tops and even little tops to cover the ends of the huge plastic straws. Big Gulp Champagne, we call it, and it's become an Imaginary Dog Awards favorite. We'll save something special—French fries, in the most recent instance—and watch the stars pick up where we left off the night before, she and I in our camp chairs, the dogs lying underfoot. Oona will have her current journal open in her lap and we'll look up at the night and contemplate Orion or Cassiopeia or Draco and think about the weeks of camping and start drinking champagne and handing out awards and she'll write them down. Our policy is that no dog goes without an award, even the (semi-coveted) Worst Camper Award.

Over the years, among the humdrum acceptance speeches for the more pedestrian awards (Best Camper, Best Sleeper, etc.) some great moments stand out: as on that memorable night in the desert, beneath the dead-black saguaros, under a crescent moon, when Bodie, our biggest and best Australian Cattle Dog pulled down the one-time "I Bit the Ranger" Award, after a playful nip to the sleeve of Ranger Steve (who's since become a friend, even dropping by our camp at the end of his shifts to see his dear friend Bodie). We'll never forget Porter the Pup winning The Avoiding the Cat on a Leash Award. There was the weeping star-struck night when Noodle, our Unknown Breed, was given the "It's Only a Fatty Tumor" Award after a trip to the vet to examine some mysterious lumps. Waddel the Red Heeler got big laughs as he accepted the Open Pit Mine award for his fine work under the picnic table, and there was Wigeon, the sainted matriarch of cattle dogs, winning the "Take Me to a Motel" Award (also known as the "I Hate the Desert" Award). But the really outstanding moment was a double award nailed down by General Douglas McBugeye, who in the High Sierra won not only the Most Improved Camper Award but followed up almost immediately with the Worst Camper Award.

The applause went wild. The fries flew over the heads of the crowd, spinning in the klieg lights. (I handle the kliegs—those little waterproof flashlights work really well.)

And here's to all the nominees. They reach high and grab their fried protein awards and they roll over and sleep, on their backs, four feet straight up, under the stars, somehow guiding human imaginations. Much better than me and the Bombshell, losing at the Grammys, riding home in the back seat of our limo, but—wait a minute—having spent the rest of the night four feet away from the best Bluegrass musicians in the world playing just for us at one of the many wonderful intimate parties you get to attend whether you win or lose, finishing off the champagne as the city lights spread below us like...yeah, wait a minute indeed, let me rethink this. It doesn't sound bad at all, and in fact, we've always had a very good time once the Bad News was announced.

Comedy is nothing if not about imagination, and if the Grammys—or even the Dog Awards—were to give out an award for Best Imaginer, I'd probably have a chance at it. And if my theories are correct, I'd trot up on stage after getting on tiptoes to kiss the Bombshell (she's very beautiful, but considerably taller than I am) and elbow whoever's up there out of the spotlight to grab the microphone and thank all my dogs, past and present. They got me there, I'd be nothing without them, etc. etc. And I'd be right. The current crop would be waiting out in the limo, asleep and dreaming, presumably, about dog food and how you'd imagine something called the Imaginary Grammy Awards in order to get more. Oona and I would wave goodbye to Ricky Skaggs and Allison Krauss and collapse into the limo, clutching our statuette and pull out the Big Gulps and pop the champagne and tell the nice driver to go slow and get up into the hills so we could hold hands and watch the city lights spread out below.

Ah, imagination. Ah, dog food.

Yesterday's News
A Tale of the Old Detective

✿

I peered over the fragrant jasmine that climbed up the rickety gate outside his Hollywood bungalow. June-bugs the size of small airplanes whirred through the twilight. When they hit the patio, they spun angrily on their backs, buzzing crazily in the sultry sunset of a South California evening.

"Walk into my world, sucker," said his voice from somewhere on the little veranda. "Drop off your coupe at Porky's Park-and-Weep across the Boulevard of Tears and try *your* luck dodging the doomed and the damned and the dead and the..." His old voice paused. He was searching, I figured, for another word that began with "d".

"Demented?" I suggested, but he didn't seem to hear me. I peered closely now and could just see him in the big rattan chair, hunched over and gesticulating, talking to himself. My elderly friend seemed swept up in some grand emotion.

"Take the little side alley called Furniture Street and climb the thirteen worn steps alongside the faded magazine stand in the dingy lobby. At the top of the stairs you'll find a door. And where you find a door, you're bound to find a doormat. Yeah, that's me, pal, face down on the linoleum."

I coughed gently and swung open the gate.

"You'll pardon me," I said, "but what you're saying has all the earmarks of an old Radio Drama, replete with the stunning exaggerations of that peculiar style of writing." I was trying to be complimentary.

"Yeah?" he said. "You're so smart? Sit down. I'd like to tell you a little story, and it's all about a…dame." He looked pleased. I knew why. Dame started with "d." There was something arch and stagy about my old friend, he whom I call the Old Detective in deference to his wish to avoid old enemies from old days in our town, which is the town mostly of Hollywood, which never likes to admit that it's old. I had never seen him quite like this before. His eyes rolled and the tones of his voice were sonorous. He knew I could scarcely resist his invitation this day. There had been few stories about him flowing from me in recent months.

"Yesterday," he announced, "people just lived in caves, that's what this dame said. 'It wasn't in the papers,' she said. 'It was too important for that. It's yesterday's news.'"

He paused and looked at me carefully. Hoping not to appear entirely stupid, I asked him what he was talking about.

"Yesterday," he announced, "people listened to the radio."

"This dame listened to the radio?" I asked.

"You're not following me," he intoned. "Yesterday was the day when people listened to the radio and yesterday itself, it turned out, was on the radio."

I thought I was losing my mind.

"Between you and me," he plunged on, "I only saw what she meant after she shot me. It had to do with the radio. You're too young, you wouldn't remember. It used to be that nothing ever happened that was really important unless it was on the radio. And yesterday was on the radio too, it was that important. When I met this dame, I finally figured out that the only way you remember anything important is if you let it get to yesterday and see if you remember it. If you do, it's important. So yesterday is like this place where you let memories go to see if they're important enough to be memories. And yesterday—where it is—is on the radio. That's where it is, that's its location. See?"

"Are you kidding?" I said. "No, I don't see. Albert Einstein couldn't see what you're talking about."

"Well, anyway," he grunted. "You've got to admit that nothing's really important unless it comes back out of yesterday and bites you, so to speak."

"Or shoots you," I said. He grunted in affirmation.

"You got that right, " he said. He got out some playing cards and set us up to sip a little bourbon out of juice glasses with pictures of the Flintstones on them. The chance I always took on my visits was that once I got there, he might not want to talk to me at all. Sensing my opportunity, I casually edged over to where my coat lay with a notebook inside. I could tell he was watching me and I thought I discerned a faint air of approval.

"That's all pretty big news to me," I said. "I never heard before that you'd ever been shot."

"Well, you probably won't understand this either," he said. "It might be big news to you, but in fact it was only old news. It wasn't much, it turned out. It only made the papers. It didn't get on the radio."

I asked him if he meant that it hadn't actually hit him.

"I told you I wound up in the hospital," he growled. "If you read the paper, there it was, 'Detective Shot' it said. Ho hum. Stop the presses. But there was nothing there about the people living in caves. This dame lived in a cave. However, if you had access to yesterday's news, there it all was."

"Why?" I asked, because I couldn't for the life of me think of anything else to say.

"Because it was on the radio. Somewhere. Somewhere, they had news on the radio, news about yesterday. It was interesting. I heard it once. Yesterday's news," he said. "That's what we're talking about, isn't it?"

"Okay," I said.

"Now, old news is just old newspapers, stackable, burnable, nothing to do with yesterday's news. Yesterday's news is alive and vital, but it's about yesterday—which isn't the day before or the day before that. Is this too technical for you? And then there was this dame involved and there was something timeless about her. But on the other hand, she was a knockout."

I was losing track. I asked him what we were talking about exactly? What did dames in caves have to do with getting shot? And what did any of it have to do with news? And this thing about yesterday was beyond me.

"Are you kidding? Are you that dense? Remember the flaming gasbag? The elephants across the Alps? The guy who ran the wrong way for a touchdown? The dame that invented radium? The little girl in the mine shaft? People living in caves? Comes rushing back fast, don't it?"

I thought to myself. "Yesterday?" I asked.

"You got that right." He seemed extraordinarily pleased with himself. "It was all in yesterday's news, sure enough, and yesterday, it turns out, was just one hell of a day. If I cared what you looked like, I'd tell you not to look so surprised. But luckily, looks don't matter."

I thought for another minute. "You mean on the radio?"

"Smart boy. Yeah, on the radio."

"You mean part of yesterday's news was that people used to listen to the radio, is that what you mean?"

"I mean right now," he said. "Isn't this on the radio?"

I told him that it wasn't so far as I knew. He was silent for a long minute, glowering. An inch-long ash hung off the end of his cigarette. I hoped I hadn't been too abrupt and asked him to just start at the beginning and tell me how the case had begun.

He paused and then with a sigh—as if it were all too much for him— he started up again. "Well, it was years ago. It was a different time. A bad time. They had Tommy Guns then that were so good they could not only search out and hit guys named Tommy, but guys named Tom or Thomas as well. They had blackjacks, back then. It was a corrupt and dark time. And they used to have a thing called "the mail" where guys in uniforms would deliver stuff right to your door."

"You're kidding," I said.

"Nope," he said sagely. "That was how I got the mystery letter that put me on the case. My mailman was named Tommy in those days and I thanked him just before he went down in a hail of bullets. I opened up the letter and inside there was nothing but a piece of the classified page from a yellowed newspaper, ripped out so you couldn't see the date or the name of the rag. I still remember what it said:

SERVICES—Caves Painted. Bulls, elks, smudges, horned sheep, handprints (your hand?); concentric circles or those other kind of circles that spiral around. Ochre. Charcoal. Peckings. Also, caves cleaned, dog food for sale. Nice firewood, some Manzanita. Radio Crystals for sale. Hollywood Boulevard, past the Flying Horse Station.

…and then down below it there was this phone number circled with charcoal or something. It was a Hollywood exchange, I could tell because this was in the days when phone numbers started with a kind of alphabetical code."

"You're kidding," I said.

"Nope," he said. "It was primitive. To dial a phone number you had to remember if it was a HEmlock number or a MElrose number or so forth. This number was one of the old ones in the HOpeless Exchange, which was the area around Hockney Canyon in the Hollywood Hills, I think. So I called it up and let it ring and then a voice answered, sweet and kind of tentative at first, but full of something special. It was a dame and she had a voice that was like the first whisper of bright color in the fall wind, a voice that made even the electricity in the phone wires want to bundle up with hot chocolate and a good book."

I mentioned that nowadays we had female voices that seemed overpowering, female FM disc jockeys for instance, and voiceover actresses selling cars on TV who sounded like adorably clever little girls.

"Yeah," he said. "Well, this one had some voice, that's what I mean to say. She sounded scared, see, but brave at the same time and the best part about it was she wouldn't tell me why. In fact, she said she wouldn't tell me anything. I asked her to at least give me her name and she finally said her name was Deedee."

I stopped him, as gently as I could, and asked him if he thought this was her actual name or was it just something convenient that started with "d."

"Look, I don't make this stuff up, you know? This actually happened, for instance. Here, look at this." With that, he pulled open his bathrobe—the fuzzy one with the little blue elephants on it—and showed me a ragged rip of a yellowish scar across his aged belly.

"Wow," I said. "It looks as real as anything."

"It's the actual scar from where she shot me. And Deedee D. D'Oppelwinn was her actual name, or so she said. And then she started talking fast and low and told me to get out to her place on the double because there was a guy trying to make her do things against her desire. The phone went dead."

I told him it certainly sounded exciting and asked him what he did next.

"Well, nothing. You see, in those days, making a dame do things against her will wasn't exactly a crime. In fact most of the time we just called it marriage." He waited for me to laugh and I didn't.

"So," he said grumpily, "I didn't do anything about it for a day. But I couldn't forget her voice. It lived inside my brain. There was something vulnerable about it. The next day, the voice was still there, in my head, and I figured I'd take a chance and drive on out to the place in the classified ad and take a look-see for myself." He leaned forward in his chair. "Now, get this," he said in a strange manner, "the guy at the Flying Horse gas station only charged me two cents a gallon for ethyl. He even tipped his hat to me. I felt like I was being flung backward into time. See? I could maybe, dimly, remember a time when gas was twenty-five cents a gallon, days when I was so flush I could afford to hire some mug to tip my hat for me, but those days—get it?—were long gone."

I asked if he didn't mean they were yesterday's news. He looked at me with some contempt.

"You just don't get it, do you? It's got to be something big to make it into yesterday's news. You're thinking of old news, which is small change. Forgotten stuff. History, for instance. You see, living in caves was one of those things that was big enough to be in yesterday's news and when I looked at the classified ad again I figured that there was a good chance that this dame lived in a cave. There was something primitive about her voice anyway and something primitive about her lack of knowledge about why she had even sent me the mystery letter. I was shaking, I swear to God. I followed the pump jockey's directions and headed fast out toward where Hollywood Boulevard dead-ends into those cotton fields, you know where that is?"

I asked him if he meant Waddle Park, figuring he couldn't because nowadays it's all multi-million dollar mansions with big gates and guys named Sean hanging around to beat you up if you stop and ask where

OJ lives. I told him I never heard about any cotton fields on Hollywood Boulevard.

"Huh. You're too young." He had a sentimental look to him. "It was cotton only yesterday. And big weeping willow trees. The jockeys used to sing like angels as they smashed the cotton, or whatever it is you do to cotton."

"Gin," I said.

"Oh, no you don't," he said and laid down a straight flush with a flourish. I told him I didn't mean the cards and we weren't playing gin anyway. He looked up at me.

"You think you're so smart," he said. "You think I don't know what a cotton gin is. We used to drink that stuff 'til the cows came home. And when the cows did come home we'd have a couple more snorts on them."

I let it pass.

"Now, when I got to the dead end all I could see was the endless fields of cotton, stretching all the way to Alabama, presumably, and an old rundown plantation house with white pillars holding up the porch and broken shutters and a general air of faded gentility about it. It had a rusting tin roof, and there was a cow tethered outside but I didn't see anything that looked like a cave. To have a cave, you see, you need some kind of a hill and this place was flat as a pancake. To have a cave in a flat place is only to have a hole. I parked my heap anyway and edged up the creaky old steps and knocked at the creaky old door. This isn't radio, right? Or the sound effects guys could just put the creaks right in and I wouldn't have to even mention it."

"Listen, I'll see what I can do about getting us on the radio," I said, trying to keep any hint of enthusiasm out of my voice.

"Great. So we'll just count this as a rehearsal. We'll pay ourselves a day of rehearsal through AFTRA," he said, as if congratulating himself. He stood up suddenly. There was the horrible crunch of a June-bug or two underfoot. He took on a sepulchral air, in the manner of someone telling ghost stories to children by the light of a campfire. He hovered over me, gesticulating.

"So, the door opens real creaky and she sticks her head out. She's something to look at, this one, I thought to myself. She was a dime-store redhead with a spray of freckles across her cute little nose, couldn't have been more than five and a half feet tall, had on those pumps or whatever you call them that made her feet seem like two packages wrapped up for a little girl's birthday party. Oh, yeah, and she was painted blue all over with some red ochre marks slashed across her apple cheeks. Other than the shoes, she didn't seem to have much of anything on at all."

I asked him if that was unusual for the times.

"Of course it was unusual. Between you and me, she looked like she lived in a cave. 'What do you want?,' she says and I says 'You sent me a letter yesterday,' and she looks frightened and whispers, 'Yesterday we lived in caves' and then she slams the door in my face. I could hear a radio on, somewhere inside. I had a thought. I knocked again and when she opened I said 'I'm here about the cave paintings,' and she says, 'Our cave is already painted, my good man, thank you very much' and then she says, 'Go away now,' and I had a brilliant idea and I says, 'No, I came to see about getting *my* cave painted, because it's all smudgy in there what with fires and not much ventilation and it looks dingy and the ritual elks the previous owner had painted are nearly smudged away what with the ravages of time.' And then this dame looks at me funny and says—get this—'That's yesterday's news, pal,' and slams the door in my face again. Isn't that great?"

I asked him what it was that was exactly so great about that, at the same time writing as fast as I could.

"Because she seemed to be using the phrase in a strictly technical manner, that's what I thought."

"Yesterday's news," I said.

"Yesterday's news. Right. I figured she meant *precisely* yesterday's news, get it? My mind was racing. What was on that radio in the background, see? I knew I had to get inside and listen and the cave thing wasn't working. I yelled that I needed to listen to her radio and she opened the door real quick and took a shot at me. It grazed me across the belly, but it didn't knock me down and so I aimed a punch at her delectable solar plexus."

"Wait, you're going too fast," I said, writing furiously. "The gun went off..."

"Yeah. Nothing happened, except it hurt like hell and my shirt got that wounded look they're so fond of in the movies. I was tempted to yell out that she'd winged me, creased me, you know. But there was nobody to hear. There were no onlookers, if you understand my meaning."

I told him that of course I knew what an onlooker was.

"On radio programs they often have small studio audiences in to watch the broadcast," he said quickly. "Is that the reason we're not on the radio, that we don't have a small studio audience?"

I told him no and tried to steer the conversation back to the gunshot. I reminded him that he had earlier said that the gunshot was only old news.

"On the radio they used to do gunshots by banging a flat stick on a table real hard."

"Just get on with it," I said grimly. He smiled.

"Okay. I ducked and swung for her delectable solar plexus, did I say that?"

"Yes," I said. "'Delectable' starts with 'D.'"

"It was like Daffy Duck," he smiled. " I whirled around twice and found myself holding her up close. Instead of decking her, I wound up kissing her right on her ruby lips. She dropped the gun real slow and lifted up one shapely calf like dames do in the movies when they kiss and she melted into me and pressed her little blue body close to mine and hung on and kissed me again, real good, and whispered that she didn't want to paint caves anymore, because ever since Big Pappy had moved up into Big Pappy's Plantation House, she never wanted to see a cave again ever in her whole life. She said painting caves was just a plain bush-league activity for a woman with some spirit and ambition. She stepped back into the light. She looked great. She said she figured Big Pappy would be out at the transmitter for another twenty minutes or so. She said she was a modern girl. She shook her hair down to her shoulders and said she was sorry she'd shot me and I said 'Don't worry, it's just a flesh wound,' and she asked me what other kind of wound there was and I couldn't answer. She was smoking a Lucky Strike and she got us a couple of martinis—it didn't take but a minute—and we engaged in some tough, quick dialogue, like detectives and dames used to know how to do. After a cigarette and a shower, there was still five minutes left. She was in the bathroom and I held onto my side and pushed open another door and could finally hear what was on her radio. It was in the kitchen. Oh, it was the real thing, all right. There it was, all the stuff of yesterday."

I asked him if he meant radium and gasbags and caves and elephants and he said yes.

"It was all there," he said. "Yesterday, laid out for you in a format as easy to listen to as Mutual News. One of the best things was that they would cut away for ads every once in a while and the products were things like clabbered milk and wigs and corn smut and slave trade futures and ochre and togas and elephant harnesses. Guys with deep voices then gave you the up-to-the-minute on everything that was happening in yesterday's news. It made you wish you were there. Then Deedee hit me over the head. I woke up in the hospital."

I told him I thought he had said he was in the hospital because of the gunshot.

"I didn't say that," he said. "I said the gunshot was in the papers. It was old news. Detectives get shot every day around here." He paused a great and weighty pause. "I never made the big time," he said sadly. "I'm old news, even now. Leave me alone. Get out of here. Leave me alone with my insufficient memories." He closed his old eyes then and put his head back and looked for all the world as if he had fallen asleep. I downed both glasses of bourbon and tucked a blanket around his lap and put my notebook in my pocket and let myself out.

I went down to the library later and searched back through the records and found an ad in an old microfilm newspaper for a fried chicken palace called "Big Pappy's Plantation House of Chicken and Waffles" that advertised live radio broadcasts on Saturday mornings. The vocalist with the band was called Deedee O'Day and the band itself was called Pappy's Primitive Palookas. I drove out Hollywood Boulevard to ask some questions but got hit in the side of the head by some guy who told me to mind my own business. There were no cotton fields, needless to say, only office buildings and billboards with ads for Korean Vodka and Japanese Beef. I decided to give up and just write up what the Old Detective had told me. It's better that way, I thought. Incomprehensible, but better.

Usually, when I get discouraged with life in our town in these makeshift modern times, the needle-point buildings swaying in the daily earthquakes and the TV filled with celebrity crimes, I've always liked to think of the Old Detective's world as the town I would want to be in if I could get back to yesterday. I close my eyes and see the old black cars humming down the boulevard past the starlets in shoulder pads and clunky heels and big hats, I see the old mugs in their old dives, guys in draped suits with fluorescent shirts and Zoot hats packing heat and the palm trees set dark against the Pacific sunsets of the past. But from what I'd now been told, that wasn't yesterday at all. It was just old news.

Well, I thought, I'd rather have it that way than thinking about our town as a place where people lived in caves, no matter how attractive and deadly they were. Maybe the trick was to get back before yesterday, back to the days when the Old Detective was young and the world wasn't cynical enough to think that yesterday's news was even something special. Remembering what I'd promised him, I turned on the radio after awhile, but the only thing on it was either people yelling at each other about Mexicans or music that sounded like it would be best enjoyed by refrigerators and toasters. I figured there was no place on it for me and my old friend and hoped he'd forget about what he'd asked me to do.

Then, suddenly the world went dark, as if there had been an eclipse of the sun. The little light left was spooky. Anything that cast a pinhole of light was in the shape of the obscured sun. From the radio, I heard the clop clop of horses' hooves on cobblestones and the cry of ancient rooks and a deep-voiced narrator talking something about Charlemagne. Then there was an ad for beaver hats, and then one for clabbered milk.

The next thing I knew, another guy with a deep voice came on and announced that the Old Detective was dead.

PHILIP AUSTIN was born in Denver, Colorado in 1941 and grew up in Fresno, California. He attended Bowdoin College, Fresno State College, and UCLA. In the 1960s he was a member of the Center Theatre Group in Los Angeles and was Program Director for Drama and Literature at KPFK-FM, where in 1966 he met his future collaborators in the Firesign Theatre—Peter Bergman, David Ossman, and Philip Proctor. The Firesign Theatre went on to write and perform more than 23 albums over 40 years, several of which featuring Austin's best-known character, Nick Danger. The group's album *Don't Crush That Dwarf, Hand Me the Pliers* was inducted into the Library of Congress' Recording Registry in 2005. As a writer he published many short stories and wrote several screenplays, including the never-produced Grateful Dead movie *Brokedown Palace* and the novel *Beaver Teeth*. He died in 2015.

Lightning Source UK Ltd.
Milton Keynes UK
UKHW020929121022
410348UK00007B/131